My Brother the Dog

By Kim Williams-Justesen

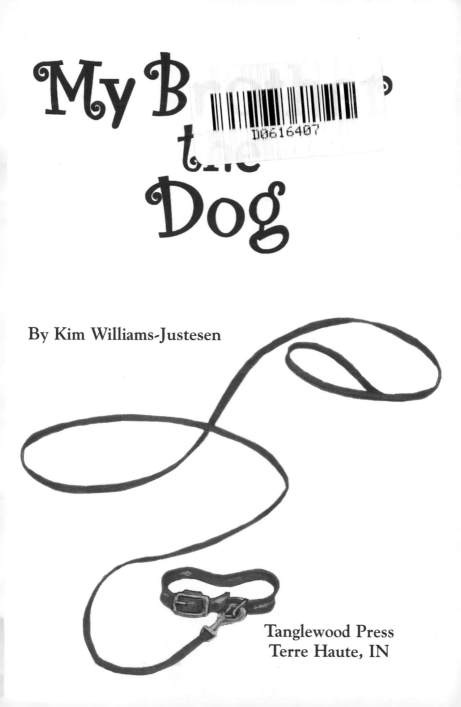

Tanglewood Press
Terre Haute, IN

Published by Tanglewood Press, LLC, May 2006.

Cover illustration by Catherine Deeter
Cover design by Gayle Force Designs
Interior design by Amy Alick Perich

The publisher would like to thank Mrs. McQueen's 8th grade class at Honey Creek Middle School for their assistance.

Tanglewood Press, LLC
P. O. Box 3009
Terre Haute, IN 47803
www.tanglewoodbooks.com

Printed in the United States of America

10 9 8 7 6 5 4 3 2 1

ISBN 0-9749303-5-0
      978-0-9749303-5-0

Library of Congress CIP data applied for.

Dedication

In addition to my wonderful husband, my sometimes darling children, and my fabulous publisher, I would like to thank some other people who helped make this dream a reality. First, my mom and her brother—the real Donny—whose retelling of such great family stories made this story come to life. Mom, you are incredible. Uncle Don, you are dearly missed. Next, to the Vermont College faculty and students for wisdom, insight, and support. Finally, to my amazing friend Jan, whose constant support keeps me going even when I don't think I can.

Chapter 1

Pop Quiz # 1

Imagine you are an average 14-year-old girl, say, like me. You are awakened one morning at 5:30 by your 4-year-old brother licking your face and barking in your ear. Your parents arrive at the sound of your screaming and respond by:

    A. asking your brother to please return to his room and play quietly so the rest of the family can continue sleeping;

    B. yelling, "What's all the screaming about, Mattie? Can't you be nice to your brother for once in your life?"; or,

    C. saying, "Wait! I gotta get the video camera for this."

B and C are how my morning started. My day seemed destined for disaster. Donny Disaster. Sounds like the perfect cartoon villain, doesn't it? Of course, if I mention this to my parents, they jump down my throat for not being nice to my little brother. And when I ask them why he can't be nice to me, my mom gives me "the eye." You know the one I mean; that squinty-eyed glare that says "drop the subject or lose a limb—your choice."

Recently Donny has decided he's a dog. Mom and Dad play along with it. If I had tried this when I was four, they would have sat me down and had a long conversation about how dogs are dogs and people are people, and I couldn't be a dog because I was a people, and I didn't have fur or a tail or paws.

But that was then, this is Donny.

Mom doesn't want to stifle his "budding creative impulses" by limiting his imagination. Dad is just convinced that everything Donny does is going to score him $10,000 on

"America's Funniest Home Videos." It has gotten so out of hand that they've even bought him a shiny red stretch collar and a nylon leash, and Mom lets him eat from a bowl on the floor.

Having managed to sneak in a few more hours of sleep after the face-licking alarm dog went off, I call my best friend Olivia, a.k.a. Livvy, to see how she is spending one of the last remaining Saturdays before school starts.

"Rearranging my room," she says. "Wanna help?"

"Love to," I say.

"Seriously?"

"Anything that gets me out of this house is a good option. What time should I be there?"

"How 'bout noon. I still need a shower and some fruity pebble cereal."

I head for the kitchen to inform my mom. She is microwaving frozen waffles for Donny, cutting them into little pieces, then drowning them in syrup and putting the bowl on the floor. I stand and stare. She never would have done this for me. Not even the frozen waffle thing. I ate all-natural, organic, pesticide-free, homemade, healthy stuff until I was ten.

But I'm not bitter or anything.

"I'm going to Livvy's in an hour," I say as Mom pours herself another cup of coffee.

"You need to get your room cleaned first and get the laundry folded before you go."

"No problemo," I say. "Anything else?"

"Take your brother," she replies.

"Mom." My voice is a bit louder than I meant for it to be, but this is clearly not fair.

"I have a hair appointment at 1:00." Her voice is not loud. It is flat and serious. I decide to argue anyway.

"I have watched him every day this summer while you and Dad were at work," I say. "Why don't I get to have one Saturday to myself? Why can't Dad watch him?" *Why can't we send him to the kennel?* I think.

"It has not been *every day*, Mattie. You don't need to be so melodramatic." Mom takes a sip of her coffee. "I told you about this when I made the appointment last week."

She *so* did not tell me. She put this off so I wouldn't get mad until it was too late.

Can you say procrastination? My mom is a champion procrastinator. She has raised procrastination to an art form.

"So leave him with Dad," I say.

"Dad had work at the office. He left earlier. I need you to watch Donny."

Hearing his name, my brother barks. He is kneeling on the floor and panting, his face covered in syrup and bits of waffle. He looks at me, pulls his arms up in front of him, and tips his head to one side. He whines, like he's begging for a treat.

"See, he wants to go with you," Mom says, smiling at him.

"This is so not fair," I say. I do not want my little brother hanging around at Livvy's. Especially when I know Nate will be there.

Just thinking of Nate makes my stomach do a little shimmy thing. Not that he even knows I breathe air. But I have hope that one day he'll see me for the goddess I hope to be by the time I'm—well—at some future date.

"Donny goes with you or you stay here." Mom dumps the rest of her coffee in the sink and heads for the back of the house.

"Arf," Donny says. He is on all fours, looking up at me and grinning.

"Mangy mutt," I say. Donny's smile wilts, and he crawls off to watch cartoons.

Cleaning my room takes about five minutes. I hate clutter, so I don't have a lot of stuff hanging around. The laundry basket is sitting on top of the dryer, overflowing with towels and sheets. Five minutes after I find the pile, it is reduced to nice fluffy stacks that are put in their respective locations. I make a pit stop in the bathroom to check the status of my hair. A little water on my fingers to scrunch the curls a bit, and I'm good to go.

Then I remember Nate. I poke around in a drawer and find a small, pink clip. I push some of the curls on the left side back and slip the clip into place.

"Cute," I say.

"Arf," says Donny.

I about jump out of my skin. I didn't hear him come down the hall.

"Brat," I say under my breath. "You better get dressed if you're going with me."

Donny takes off down the hall as fast as

he can go on all fours. The sun coming through the skylight in the hall reflects off his shiny red collar. *Could he be any weirder?*

"Mattie?" Mom calls. She has that tone in her voice that says she needs something. "Have you seen my car keys?"

All the kitchen drawers are opened. Mom is on her tiptoes, feeling around the top of the refrigerator.

"Not in your purse?"

"No, I checked already."

"On your desk?"

"No, Mattie, now will you help me look around for them?"

"Donny probably buried them in the yard again," I say.

"Already looked," Mom says. "No fresh holes in the garden." She doesn't sound as exasperated as I expect her to.

In the corner by the sofa is a big cushion that Donny uses as his bed. On a hunch, I lift the cushion. "This what you're after?" I jingle the keys and hold them up for her to see.

She smiles and laughs. "Where did he hide them, under his dog bed?"

I nod. *I would never get away with this without a lecture of some kind.*

Mom grabs the keys from me. "I've gotta dash."

I hear the groan of our automatic door. She spins around in the doorway and looks at me very directly. "Be nice to your brother. He still isn't feeling one hundred percent, so don't let him get over-tired. And make sure he gets a nap if I'm not home by 2:00."

Before I have a chance to ask her why she wouldn't be home by 2:00, the door to the garage is closed, and I can hear the car engine start.

I check the clock on the microwave: 11:30. As I step back toward the kitchen, my toes discover something smooshy and sticky.

"Donald!" I pull off the waffle piece stuck to my foot and hurry to clean up the other pieces he has left strewn on the floor. Wiping up the syrup with a cloth from the sink, I wonder how much longer this dog fantasy can last. It has been going on for more than a week now. He was bored with the toy truck two days after he got it for his birthday. The plastic dinosaur that came with his fast food lasted only a few hours. But this dog thing—well, I'm tired of it already.

Donald bounces into the kitchen, carrying his sandals in his teeth. He whimpers at me.

"Those straps just stick together," I say. You can do those by yourself."

He drops the shoes and shakes his head, pouting at me.

"I'm not touching your slimy sandals after you've had them in your mouth. And you need to go wash your face. It's all sticky from breakfast." I know he can do all of these things. He's been doing them for nearly a year.

He sits back on his feet and starts licking his hand. Then he rubs his hand on his face. I grab the nearest dishtowel, turn on the faucet to get it wet, then start toward my brother.

"Yi - yi - yi," he yelps.

"I'll leave you here if you don't let me wash you off," I say. It's an empty threat because Mom would kill me if I left him, but

I'm hoping he doesn't figure that part out.

I grab his hands and wipe them, but when I reach for his face, he bolts.

"Get back here," I say as I chase him down the hall. He bounds into his bedroom and scrambles under his bed. The fact that he can move so fast on his knees catches me by surprise. I kneel down by the bed and try pulling him out, but he avoids my hand. He has pushed himself way into the corner, and I have to slide halfway under the bed to reach him. Just as I'm about to grab his foot, he slithers out and takes off down the hall.

"If you know what's good for you, you better get your hind end over here so I can clean you up." I back out from under the bed.

Donny is sitting on the dog bed, his eyes wide. He holds perfectly still while I wipe off his mouth and chin.

"I'm leaving. If you're coming with me, you put your shoes on by yourself." I slip on my sandals and turn to leave.

Donny has shoes on his feet and the leash in his mouth.

"No," I say. But then I realize that this might make things easier. I clip the leash to his ever-present collar, and we start walking toward Livvy's.

Chapter 2

Pop Quiz #2

Imagine you are me again. You are shopping at the mall for back-to-school clothes, and your little brother starts gyrating and making all kinds of annoying sounds. Your mother and father insist that you escort him to the ladies' room while they finalize their purchases. Totally humiliated, you show him where the men's room is and wait patiently out by the food court. After a few minutes, your parents arrive and demand to know where their son is, just as your little brother emerges from the restroom, minus his pants. He proceeds to run through the food court, butt-naked, while you chase him around. Your parents respond by:

A. scooping up the little streaker, securing his clothing, and giving you an extra $50 to ease your embarrassed soul with some additional clothes;

B. yelling, "Why'd you let him go in there by himself? Go in there and get his pants before he catches his death of cold"; or,

C. saying, "Wait, I've gotta get the video camera for this."

The answer is not A. I'm reviewing this and similarly embarrassing moments courtesy of Donny Disaster as we make our way to Livvy's house in the late August heat. One of our less environmentally aware neighbors has his sprinklers on—like it will actually do any good at high noon—and Donny is tugging at his leash, wanting to romp through the water.

"Forget it," I say. I keep a firm grip on the leash.

Donny whimpers and pulls harder.

"Look," I say, "we're almost there, and they have central air conditioning. Besides," I add, "Mom will kill me if I let you get wet and you get sick again."

Donny relents. He continues to plod along beside me. He gave up walking on all fours a few blocks ago because he was scuffing his knees and getting gravel in his paws. We get to Livvy's, and I'm about to ring the doorbell when Donny barks.

"Arf," he says. "Arf, arf, arf," like some yappy little dog the size of a football. The kind of dog you want to pick up and see how far you can punt it.

"Here," I say, handing the leash to my brother. "Hold Donny and don't let him run away."

The stupid kid holds out his hand, then he stands there on the steps, holding himself by the leash.

"Hey, Mattie, what's up?"

It's Nate. My stomach does the shimmy thing again. "Livvy's in her room," he says and holds the screen door open for me. A blast of cool air hits me in the face as I step into the foyer. *How I covet real air conditioning.*

"What's with the kid?" Nate says, looking out at Donny.

"He's a dog," I explain.

Nate nods. "Is he house-trained?"

He smiles when I laugh, and my knees get mushy. Nate is 16, almost 17. He plays football. Defensive back. He is a god. For a moment, I forget that my brother is a dog. I forget that I have a brother.

I picture Nate in a white shirt that bares his muscular chest. He sweeps me up in his arms, carrying me off to some secluded castle on a hilltop. I feel his hands running through my hair, caressing my face. I feel his warm breath as he kisses my neck. I feel him sniff my ankles.

My Harlequin moment shatters around me. Donny is sniffing my ankles. I want to kill him.

"Bark," says Donny.

"Stay," I say. He sits down inside the doorway, still holding the leash.

Nate chuckles and wanders off. I follow him with my eyes, then climb the stairs to Livvy's room. Music pumps from behind her bedroom door. I can hear her singing—

sort of. Livvy can't carry a tune in a bucket. She can't carry a tune in a dump truck. I knock on the door.

Nothing.

I bang on the door.

"What," she yells.

"Stop torturing those cats," I yell back.

The door flies open. "Chica," she says, putting her hands lightly on my shoulders and doing the Hollywood kiss-kiss-in-the-air thing. "Come on in, the water's fine."

I step into the chaos Livvy calls her room. Multicolored beads hang from the ceiling. A lava lamp bubbles on the night-stand, and a mini disco light is spinning on top of her dresser. Her bed is piled with something that I'm sure her mother calls linens.

"Can you turn it down?" I say.

"The music?"

"No, the pot roast. Duh." I plug my ears to try and keep from going prematurely deaf. The thumping subsides to a moderate throb.

"I thought little Donny dude was com-ing with you," Livvy says as she walks over the top of her bed to the window on the far side of her room.

"He did," I say. "He's sitting in the foyer by the door."

"Why?"

"Because I told him to stay." I watch as Livvy scrapes an old sticker off her window with a nail file.

"Why?" she says.

"Because that's what dogs do," I say. "They sit. They stay."

Livvy turns to look at me. "Huh?"

"Did I not tell you this?" I'm sure that I must have mentioned it before now. "Donny is a dog. At least, this week he's a dog. Next week who knows? He might be a cat, or a cow, or a ring-tailed lemur."

"Your little brother totally rocks," she says. She turns back to the sticker removal project. Little pieces of brightly colored paper fall in curls on the windowsill as she works. "So you wanna help me rearrange furniture?" she asks.

"It would be an honor and a pleas. . . well . . . let's just stick with honor for now."

She scrapes the last of the sticky part of the sticker from the window, then sweeps

the remnants from the sill onto her floor.
I shudder.

"Toss the stuff off my bed into the hall,"
Livvy says. "Then we can finish rearranging."

"I didn't realize you'd started yet." I look
around the room.

"Ha ha," she says. "I reorganized all my
drawers already and cleaned my closet."

I look toward her closet. The door is
closed and I decide it's better to take her
word on it instead of checking for myself.

"Don't believe me?" she asks. She climbs
over the bed again and slides the closet
door open. I cover my eyes, completely
scared of what may be hidden inside. Then
I peek between my fingers and let out a
loud gasp.

"You didn't think I was serious." Livvy
sounds genuinely hurt. Then she grins.

I gather up the jumble of sheets and
blankets and toss them into the hall.
"What goes where?"

"I wanna turn my bed around and put it
over there." Livvy points to the corner by
the window. "Then I want my dresser over
there." She points to the corner on the

opposite side of the window. "Then I'll
have all this floor space, and it'll feel like
my room is ten times bigger." She spreads
her arms out wide.

"How feng shui," I say.

Livvy moves to the head of her bed and
starts tugging.

"Don't you want to vacuum first?"

She looks at me like I've suddenly started speaking Swahili.

"You know, vacuum? Clean the floor?" I
move my arm back and forth to demon-
strate.

"What for? I can do it after I move the
bed."

I shrug, move to the opposite end, and
help her shove the bed into its new position against the far wall. We discover an
interesting collection of furry stuff under-
neath where her bed used to be.

"So, that's where that went," Livvy says,
picking up a dust bunny-covered sports bra.
She tosses it at me and I duck.

The doorbell rings, and Livvy peers out
the window. In a flash she is at the dresser,
pulling clothes out and tossing them on the

unmade bed.

"Something wrong?" I ask. I head to the window and look outside. A green Jeep sits in the driveway.

"Chris," Livvy says, her voice a flustered hush. "Chris's here. Chris's here."

"You are *so* pathetic."

She changes clothes in a rapid-fire motion that makes me dizzy. Now she wears a cotton skirt and a pink tie-dye shirt. "Is this good? Or should I wear the red tee-shirt with the denim shorts?" Without waiting for a reply, she changes again.

"Have you gone bananas?" I ask. "Chris doesn't even know you breathe air, so he most certainly isn't going to notice what tee-shirt you've got on."

Livvy pauses and looks at me. "Thanks for your support." She grabs a brush off the top of her dresser and maneuvers her long hair into a ponytail. She fastens it with a big silver clip, then spins around to look at me again. "So?"

"So?" I say.

"Let's go see what those boys are up to," she says. She gets this devious grin on her face that makes me a little nervous. It reminds me of the time she talked me into calling Michael Cummings and pretending I was another girl, trying to find out if he liked Livvy or not. I'm just not good at lying or pretending to be someone I'm not.

A door in the kitchen leads to the garage. Livvy tiptoes over and presses her ear against it. Even from where I'm standing, I can hear noise coming from the other side.

"They're working on the Mazda," she says. A loud, metallic clanking confirms her statement. "Want a Popsicle?" she says. She nods toward the garage where their storage freezer is. My knees start to feel wobbly again.

"Livvy, don't go out there and bug them."

"I'm not bugging them," she says. "I'm getting Popsicles for us and for your brother."

She twists the knob, motions for me to follow, then opens the door. I walk quickly behind her, feeling like a total goon. I stand frozen on the steps that lead to the garage. The faint smell of grease and gasoline hangs in the air. I notice a little extra sway in Livvy's hips as she moves past the midnight blue Mazda sitting on blocks. The hood is raised and Nate is bent over the engine. He looks at Livvy and me, his face streaked with oil and sweat. Even grungy, he's gorgeous.

"Just getting a treat," Livvy says as she opens the freezer door. "You guys want one?"

Nate practically glares at her. "We can get our own, thanks." He sounds like he's rather annoyed at the interruption. Chris looks like he might start to laugh.

Livvy heads back toward me, five or six Popsicles in her hands. "Let me know if you change your mind," she says.

I follow her to the kitchen and take up residence on a stool near the counter. Livvy tears the paper away from a grape Popsicle, and I unwrap a lime one.

"Do you think he noticed?" she asks.

"That you're a complete dweeb?" I say. "Yeah, he noticed."

She throws the wrapper at me.

"It's not my fault you're pathetic," I say, throwing the wrapper at her.

"No more pathetic than you," she says.

"Meaning?"

"Meaning I saw you drooling over my

brother, chica," she says.

"I wasn't."

"Were too," she says. "Speaking of 'he doesn't even know you breathe air'."

Even though I know she's right, it still stings to hear it. I have known Livvy since third grade. Her brother was in fifth. He has been making my knees wobbly ever since I first saw him on the playground.

"I grabbed one for Donny," Livvy says. "What flavor does he like?"

"Depends," I say, looking toward the front door. "Donny," I call. Livvy puts the extra Popsicles in the freezer as I head toward the door. "Donny," I call again. "Want a Popsicle?"

No response.

Livvy joins me in the foyer. "Is this where you parked him?"

"Yeah," I say. I look around for signs of my brother.

"He probably got bored," she says.

"That's what I'm afraid of." I don't even want to think of where he might have gone. Or what he might be doing.

I walk back toward the kitchen, then

into the dining room at the rear of the house. "Donny, knock it off and come here."

"Hey, little dude," Livvy calls. "I've got a Popsicle for you."

I run back to the foyer and open the door. The heat presses on me as I step outside. "Donny," I call at the top of my lungs. I look up and down the sidewalk, across the street. No sign of him. Nothing.

I walk back to the house. Livvy is standing by the stairs.

"Great," I say. "I've lost my dog."

Chapter 3

Livvy and I run through the house, calling for my brother. My heart pounds loudly in my ears. "Maybe he went home," Livvy says.

"I don't think he knows the way without me." *Not that I think that would keep him from leaving.*

"I'll go ask Nate if he's seen him," Livvy says. I jog up the stairs to see if he's hiding under a bed or in the linen closet. Donny likes squeezing himself into the smallest spaces he can find. He thinks it makes him "inbizibo" —he's almost right.

I feel weird looking through Mr. and Mrs. Byer's room, but it would be just like Donny to hide in their closet. I get on the floor and

look under their bed. Nothing but slippers
and darkness. I open their closet door.

"Donald George," I say in my most
stern, big sister voice. "If you're in there,
you are in deep, doggy doo-doo." I push
aside the dresses and pants, and shirts
draped in plastic from the dry cleaners.
They make a soft rustling sound, but no
barking. Then I get an idea.

I step into the hallway at the top of the
stairs, pretty sure my voice will carry
through the top floor. "Here Donny, here
boy," I say. I whistle. "Wanna treat boy?" I
wait. Nothing. I head down stairs and stand
in the tiled foyer. "Here Donny, here boy." I
whistle again and slap my leg. "Come here
boy, come get a treat."

From the garage, I can hear laughter.
The door slams and Livvy stomps into the
kitchen. "Buttheads," she says.

"I've got an idea," I say.

Livvy looks at me, confusion scribbled
across her face.

"Here Donny, here boy," I say. I slap my
hand on my leg again. "Here boy, come get
a treat."

Livvy smiles and nods. "Here dude, here Donny," she calls.

We go through the main floor, then move outside and start to circle around the house. We reach the back just as I'm about to give in to panic. I whistle again.

"Wanna treat?" Livvy calls.

"Bark," comes the response.

"Come here, Donny," I say. "Come get your doggy treat."

From out of the bushes comes a mud-covered, stickery-tangled mess. A mess with a shiny red collar and a leash.

"Hey, little dude, you been burying bones?" Livvy looks entertained. I am not at all amused.

Donny sits back on his haunches, sticks out his tongue, and pants. He nods. "Arf," he says.

"I guess that takes care of the rest of my afternoon," I say. I grab the leash. "I have to take him home and give him a bath."

"Yi-yi-yi," whines Donny.

Livvy laughs. "I don't think he's too hip on that idea."

"Yeah, well, tough dog biscuits. If Mom

comes home and sees him like this, I'll be grounded until school starts." I look my brother right in his dirt-streaked face.

"We could just turn the hose on him," Livvy says.

I can't decide if she's trying to be funny, or if she really thinks that would work. Sometimes it's hard to tell with Livvy.

"I'll pass, thanks," I say. I tug on Donny's leash and he makes a growling noise. Part of me would like to drag him. I look at Livvy. "Come with me and help, okay? You can entertain him while I get him cleaned up."

"Beats rearranging furniture," she says. "Let me tell Nate. I'll meet you up front."

"Come on Donny," I say. He doesn't move.

"Donny, come on. I gotta get you cleaned up before Mom comes home and yells at me."

He looks up at me, tilting his head to one side. He blinks at me.

"Please, Donny," I beg. "Please start walking." Donny stays put.

"Look," I say, resorting to bribery, "if

you'll cooperate, you can have a Popsicle for the walk home, and another one when you get out of the bathtub."

Donny smiles and nods. He pops up and starts gallop-running toward the front of the house, dragging me behind him. He sits on the steps by the door, pants, and looks up at me.

"What flavor Popsicle do you want?" I ask.

"Bark," he says.

"I don't know what flavor 'bark' is, unless you plan to eat a tree."

"Bark," he says again.

I let out a long sigh. "Fine, you get what I give you."

"Gwape," he says. It's the first human word he's used all day. I'm grateful.

"Don't go anywhere," I say as I walk inside to get his treat. I grab a purple Popsicle and hurry back before Donny has a chance to slip away again.

Livvy emerges from the garage. "We are adios," she says.

I unwrap the Popsicle and twist the paper around the stick. No sense adding sticky to muddy. I hand it to Donny, who immediately shoves it in his mouth.

"I wish I had a little brother," Livvy says. "It would be fun."

"Yeah, right," I say.

"Seriously. I think it would be a blast. Your little brother totally rocks."

"You don't live with him."

Livvy kicks at a piece of gravel. "Yeah, well, I wish I did."

I'm about to offer her a trade, her brother for mine, but I decide against it. "It's got to be at least a hundred out here," I say, changing the subject.

Livvy looks up at the sky. "I can't believe that summer's almost over."

"Me either."

"I can't believe we're going to be freshmen," she says.

"Me either."

We walk a little way in silence, then she says. "Are you, like, scared to go to high school?"

"Nervous, maybe," I say. "Not really scared."

Livvy lets out a sigh. "Hmm."

"Are you?" I ask.

"A little," she says. "Everybody there knows Nate. Everybody there loves Nate. I'm just his geeky little sister."

"That should give you instant credibility," I say. "Think of all the guys who will want to hang with the football star's sister."

Livvy shrugs. "I somehow doubt that's how it'll be."

"Yeah, well, at least they'll know you breathe air."

Livvy smiles at me. "Nate will convince them I don't. He'll convince them I'm a toad."

"He wouldn't."

"Bet me."

"Nate's not a bully." My voice sounds a bit more defensive—and fourth grade—than I intended. But I can't believe that he would be that mean. Not to his own sister.

"You don't live with him," Livvy says.

We reach my house and go through the front door. The window cooler in the kitchen chugs its little heart out, but it still feels like it's about 98 degrees inside. I remind myself to ask Santa Claus and the Easter Bunny for central air conditioning.

"Let's get him in the tub," I say.

Donny runs ahead of us, slamming the door to his room. I turn on the faucet and check the temperature.

Livvy sits on the bathroom counter, leaning against the big mirror. "So, this dog thing. . ."

I brush my wilted curls back from my eyes. "Yeah, I know. He's weird."

Livvy laughs. "No, I think it's funny."

"It's not so funny at 5:30 in the morning."

Livvy's eyes go wide, and she slaps her hand over her mouth like she might scream. She points behind me, and I turn to discover Donny standing in the hallway. He is completely naked except for his dog collar and leash.

"Come here," I say, taking off the leash. I start to take off the collar, but Donny wraps both hands around it and shakes his head.

"Suit yourself," I say. I lift his mostly muddy body into the tub and proceed to scrub. Donny thrashes around, splashing water everywhere. I'm dripping wet, and Livvy is in hysterics behind me. My jaw clenches.

"This isn't funny," I say, but she keeps laughing. Donny realizes that his splashing makes Livvy laugh, so he thrashes and splashes even more. Water droplets slide down the walls.

"Stop it," I yell, but it doesn't matter. The more he splashes, the more Livvy laughs. The more Livvy laughs . . .

"Donald, knock it off right now!" I grab him by both arms and hold him tight. He freezes. Tears well in his eyes, and he starts to cry. I grab the plastic bowl that Mom uses to wash Donny's hair and fill it with water. Without warning, I dump it over his head. He howls, but I don't care. I just want to get him clean and get myself dry before Mom gets home.

I scrub his head with baby shampoo and dump another bowl of water on him to rinse the suds. He screams and rubs his eyes.

"It doesn't sting," I say.

"Foap eye," Donny cries. "Foap eye."

"The soap doesn't sting your eyes," I say. "It's the same one Mom uses."

Livvy hops down and sits next to me. "Don't be so harsh," she says.

"If he isn't going to cooperate, I don't have much choice," I say. But I look at Donny, his lower lip sticking out in a frightened pout, and my heart sinks a little that I was so rough with him.

"Hey, dude, you want me to style your hair?" Livvy grabs the conditioner and squeezes some into her hand. Donny nods, but he won't look up. I feel like a first-class schmuck now.

"Great," I say. "He holds perfectly still for you, but he practically drowns me."

"That's 'cause he knows I'm the best doggy groomer in town," Livvy says.

"Bark," says Donny. He looks up at Livvy and smiles, his eyes red from crying and rubbing.

"I'm gonna go put some dry clothes on," I say.

Livvy massages her fingers in Donny's hair, then wraps it into a twist that stands up like a horn.

"Nice height," she says.

I change clothes and head to Donny's room to look for clean stuff for him to wear. As I rifle through his dresser drawers for

something clean, I can hear Donny and
Livvy giggling in the bathroom. I wish he
would giggle like that for me.

Livvy has Donny sitting on the counter,
wrapped in a towel, when I come in to get
him dressed. She brushes his hair to one
side and makes it stand out from his head.
He laughs and turns from side to side to
catch every angle in the mirror.

"Surfer dog," Livvy says as I put the
clothes on the counter. "Got any gel?"
she asks.

I rummage through the drawer and pull
out some glitter hair gel. "I don't think this
is a good idea," I say.

"What do you think, Donny?" Livvy asks.

"Arf," Donny says. He lets his tongue
hang out and he pants. "Arf, arf, arf."

Livvy squirts some of the pink-tinted
sparkling goop into one hand, then works it
into Donny's blonde hair. She smoothes all
his hair forward, then messes it up. She
pulls two strands into horns and twists
them so they stand on their own.

"That's appropriate," I say.

Livvy grins at me. Donny doesn't get it.

Livvy starts twisting strands all over Donny's head, making little spikes, until he looks like some kind of punked-out hedgehog. The pink glitter just makes it that much more ridiculous. I start to laugh. Donny's eyes sparkle, and his smile stretches across his whole face.

"Blow-dryer," Livvy says, like a surgeon asking for a scalpel. I grab the blow-dryer from under the sink and plug it in. She dries the pink-tinted spikes into place. We both giggle like crazy.

After a few spritzes of hair spray, Livvy lifts him from the counter and we carefully pull his shirt over his head. He steps into his Elmo undies and pulls on a pair of denim shorts. With the shiny red collar, he looks like a miniature punk rocker. Donny Rotten. I can't stop laughing, and I wipe at the tears with the back of my hand.

"Dude," Livvy says, "you are completely the most awesome dog on the planet."

Donny runs down the hall to his room, then comes back with his fist wrapped tight around something. He holds it out to Livvy. She puts out her hand, and he drops in a bunch of pennies.

"Oh no, really. No charge. You are so cool looking, that's payment enough." She gives the pennies back to him. Donny's grin is so big I think his face might crack.

Then he sneezes. I stop laughing.

"Well, bless you," Livvy says.

I look at my brother. "Are you cold?" I ask. He shakes his head. I put my hand out to feel his forehead, but he ducks and runs for his room.

"What was that all about?" Livvy asks.

"He's had this weird summer cold thing," I say. "It's been hanging around for, I don't know, a week or so?"

I pick up the towel and his dirty clothes and toss them in the hamper. "I guess he's sick of everyone trying to take his temperature and give him medicine."

"Can't say I blame him," Livvy says. She holds her hands out. They sparkle with a pink, glittery tint in the light. She turns back to the sink and starts washing.

"My mom is going to freak when she sees his hair," I say. "I'll probably be grounded—again."

"Nah. Just tell her it's my fault. She can't ground me."

"She can try."

"Yeah," Livvy says, drying her hands. "But it would be worth it. He looks totally cool with spikes." She laughs.

"Yeah," I agree, "he does."

Chapter 4

Pop Quiz #3

Okay, you are me again. You are at the
county fair with your family, your best
friend, and your best friend's stunningly
handsome older brother. Your chance to
impress the stunningly handsome older
brother arrives in the form of the Octopus
of Doom ride. Not only will he see your
adventurous side, but maybe he'll go on the
ride with you, allowing you to come into
close, physical contact with his gorgeous
self. But the fates intervene in the form of
your parents, and instead, you are forced to
ride with your own brother. As the ride

spins and whirls, your little brother starts spewing lime slushee and cotton candy like some demonic fountain. Your parents respond by:

    A. demanding that the pimple-faced attendant stop the ride immediately so they can remove their son and comfort their totally humiliated daughter;

    B. yelling, "Why aren't you helping your brother?" as the spinning arm of the Octopus flies by at 98 miles an hour; or,

    C. saying, "Wait, I've gotta get the video camera for this."

Need I tell you the answer here? It could have been the perfect opportunity. It could have been my chance to make an impression on Nate. Livvy's family was going to the fair, and Livvy invited me to come with her. I'm thinking it's the ideal way to spend a little quality time with Nate. You know, try to get him to impress me by throwing baseballs at milk bottles to win a giant, stuffed animal. So I ask if I can go, and my delirious father, who normally hates the fair, decides this would be loads of fun for Donny.

It's important to note here that my dad hates crowds. My dad hates amusement parks—he calls them "asphalt evil." My dad also can't stand the smell of barnyard animals—even the blue ribbon-winning ones. But because it's yet another opportunity to videotape Donny, it becomes a family outing.

So instead of quality time with Nate, I get drenched in second-hand slushee. Instead of carrying home a giant stuffed panda, I'm carrying the smell of my little brother's barf.

We pull into the garage and I leap from the car, race to the laundry room, and strip to my undies. Then I take the stairs two at a time to hit the shower.

The warm water and steamy air help me to relax just a little. As I scrub myself with the loofah and vanilla shower gel, I picture Nate's face the moment I dared him to ride the Octopus. Had I seen a twinkle? A glimmer of interest? A slight hint of intrigue in those oh-so-perfect brown eyes? Then I remember his expression when I got off the ride, drenched and reeking to high heaven. I had most certainly made an impression.

I wash my hair for the second time, trying to make certain there is absolutely nothing clinging to me that in any way resembles recycled cotton candy. Convinced I am now barf-free, I step out of the shower.

"Bark."

"Mom!" I scream.

I grab a towel and wrap it around me, a little embarrassed, a lot angry. Donny scootches back into the corner by the hamper.

"Ever hear of knocking?" I ask. I storm to my room, slamming the door so that everyone will know exactly what my mood is, not that I had left any doubt as we made our way home.

I get dressed, towel dry my hair, then head back to the bathroom for the blow dryer. Donny sits cross-legged on the floor outside his bedroom door. He wears a fresh set of clothes and his hair is wet. He looks up at me.

"What," I say.

"Sahwee," he says. He crawls into his

room and closes the door with a soft click. Once again, I feel like a schmuck.

I walk to his room and knock. He doesn't answer, but I twist the knob and go in anyway.

"Evo hew oh knocking?" Donny says.

"I did knock," I say softly. "You didn't answer."

"Go way."

Donny sits on the rug that looks like you are looking down on a city. It has pictures of buildings, roads, and streams. I sit on a factory and put my hand on Donny's shoulder. "I know you didn't mean to get sick," I say.

"It woh a ackident," he says.

"An accident. I know," I say, not really to correct him, but to make sure I understand. "But I tried to tell you that the Octopus ride was for big kids."

"I a big kid," Donny says. He looks me right in the eye. "I go a school."

"You go to preschool," I say. "But the Octopus is for really big kids. Like Nate. Like me. Like Livvy."

Donny looks down at his feet and plays

with the fasteners on his shoes. He peels them apart, then pushes them closed again. Open, close, open, close.

"Donny, I'm not mad at you. Okay?"

"No," Donny says.

I sit up a little straighter. Usually when I say I'm not mad, he says "okay," and we move on.

"It's okay, Donny."

"No. Not okay." Donny curls up into a little ball, still pulling the sandal strap apart, then sticking it back together.

"Why? What's not okay?"

"You not like me," he says. "You fay I fupid."

"I didn't say you were stupid."

"Yeah, you do."

"No, I didn't," I say. Actually, I might have said it when I got off the ride. Or in the car on the way home. I can't exactly remember at the moment.

Donny sniffs and wipes at his cheeks with one hand.

"I'm sorry, Donny. I don't think you're stupid. I was just angry. But I'm not angry now."

"You fink I a baby."

"You're not a baby." The words don't come out too convincing, even to me. I'm getting frustrated that he won't just accept my apology and be done with it.

Mom's voice reaches up the stairs and down the hall. "Mattie? Would you please come down here for a minute?"

This typically means I'm in trouble—again. I'm assuming it's because I yelled at Donny, or called him stupid, or something along those lines. I trudge down the stairs to the den and stand in the doorway, waiting for the barrage of "Don't call your brother names" and "Can't you be nice to him?" that I'm sure is coming.

Dad sits in the recliner, scanning the paper like there is some hidden code he needs to find. Mom sits on the sofa, her legs drawn up next to her. Her hair is combed away from her face, and she has a bandana tied like a headband across the top of her head.

"What," I say. *Here it comes*, I'm thinking. *I'm probably grounded again.*

"Mattie," Mom says, "I'm sorry about what happened on the ride. I shouldn't have let your brother go on that thing."

"Buh?" I'm too stunned for a coherent reply.

"That was just too much for him to handle, and I shouldn't have let him go on it. If you're going to be upset at someone, be upset at me, not your brother."

I stare at my mom. I wonder if my eyes are all bugged out. I wonder if this is some sort of a trap, like she's really testing my response, and if I don't say the right thing, she'll throw in the classic, "I knew it. You're grounded."

I shift my focus to Dad. He looks up from the paper and nods his agreement. He gives the paper a good shake, turns the page, and goes back to code hunting.

"Then why did you let him go?" I ask.

Mom shrugs. "Your little brother thinks you are the most wonderful person on earth. He wants to go everywhere you go and do everything you do. I know it drives you crazy sometimes."

"How about most of the time," I say. "Just once, I'd like to hang out with my friends and do something by myself, without

Hurricane Donny showing up to ruin it."

Mom's lips draw tight and I brace myself—but she lets out a long sigh. "Olivia called while you were in the shower. She wants to see if you can come over and spend the night."

I'm a little stunned at the direction this conversation is going. I have yet to be grounded, and if I'm reading this right, Mom sounds like she is about to let me go to Livvy's for a sleepover.

"I told her that would be fine with me, but that I'd have you call when you were out of the tub."

My heart does a leap in my chest. "Really?" I ask.

"I think a night off would be good for you. You've spent a lot of time helping me with Donny. After today's adventure, I think I owe you a break."

My eyes are doing the bugged-out thing again, and I feel like I have to force my lids to close and hold them in their sockets. When I open my eyes again, Mom is still looking at me with her "I'm really sorry" expression on her face.

"I'll go call Livvy," I say, but I don't move.

Dad gives the paper another firm shake. "I think there's some microwave popcorn in the cupboard. You could take it with you. Make a real party out of this."

Mom and Dad have not let me stay overnight at anyone's house all summer. Not that I've asked, now that I think about it. I guess sleepovers become less of a big deal when you're about to become a freshman.

"Better go call Livvy and give her an answer," Mom says.

I turn toward the kitchen, stop, then look at Mom and Dad. "Thanks," I say. I run and grab the phone and call Livvy.

"Hello?" Nate answers, and I momentarily forget what I was going to say.

"Hello?" he says again.

"Oh, um, hi—Nate, um, this is Mattie." *Brilliant. You sound like a moron.*

Nate chuckles. "Hey, Mattie." He laughs. "How's your little brother?"

My face feels hot. "He's fine, thanks. Can I talk to Livvy?"

"Yeah. Let me get her."

The phone at Livvy's house clatters on

the counter, and I can hear Nate yelling. Livvy picks up the extension. "Hello?"

"It's Mattie," I say.

"Hey, chica. You coming over?"

"Yeah, if that's okay."

Livvy covers the phone and yells, "Nate, hang it up, you dirt bag."

More laughing, then click.

"Sorry, Mattie, my brother's a butthead."

"So's mine," I say. "Must be the mutant Y chromosome."

"So when are you coming over?"

I look at the clock. It's 5:30. "Depends on if I'm walking, biking, or getting my dad to drive me."

"Whichever is fastest. My mom said we could order pizza and rent a movie."

Now it's my turn to cover the phone and yell. "Hey, Dad? Can you drive me to Livvy's?"

There is some muffled discussion in the den, then my dad steps into the kitchen. "Sure. I'll take you." He tucks his golf shirt back into his shorts, and I notice that he is barefoot. I immediately decide my dad has the ugliest feet in the world, and I am definitely investing in weekly pedicures when I get older.

"My dad will drive me, so I'll be there in five?"

"Cool," Livvy says. "I'll let my mom know. See you in a sec."

I head to my room to collect the important stuff, like an extra-large tee shirt, a pillow, and my fuzzy leopard print slippers. I shove these into a duffle bag from my closet and make for the cupboard. With the popcorn added to the other essentials, I slip on my sandals and head for the car. The smell of barf wafts through the air as I open the door.

"Roll down your window, would ya?" Dad says as he slips behind the wheel.

I crank the window down, then open the back door and crank that window, too. Dad leans his head out the window like a dog as we drive. I'm glad it's a short trip. I don't want any of this smell to cling to me after I scrubbed so hard to get rid of it.

The garage door is up at Livvy's, and Nate is bent over the engine of the Mazda again.

"Thanks, Dad," I say. I open the door and climb out. Dad turns off the motor and opens his door. This is not a good thing. I turn and look at him. "Yes," I say, "their parents are here. They will be here all night. We will not throw any wild parties without inviting you."

"Not worried about it," he says. He walks toward the midnight blue Mazda. I should have known. Dad is a major motorhead car geek.

He bends over the engine next to Nate. They are pointing at stuff and saying things like "crank shaft" and "headers" and "torque." I decide to find Livvy and separate myself from my dad to limit the "guilt by association" factor. My skin prickles from the cool air as I step into the kitchen.

Mrs. Byer is on the phone. "Do you like pepperoni?" she asks as I wave at her. I nod.

"With pepperoni, extra cheese, olives, and mushrooms."

I'm about to say, "Eww, not mushrooms," but I am the guest, and I should just be thankful I'm eating pizza with Livvy and Nate, not watching the Disney Channel with Donny.

Livvy comes bounding down the stairs

and lands with a thud in the foyer. She
runs across the kitchen. "Come upstairs,"
she says, grabbing my duffle bag and dragging me through the room. We are both
laughing as we head up the steps.

"Cover your eyes," she says as we get to
her door. "No peeking."

I hear the knob turn, then Livvy pulls
me by the elbow.

"Okay, now."

I look through my fingers, then drop my
hands.

"Wow," I manage. Her room is impressive. Truly impressive. Her bed is made, her
dresser is cleaned off, and there is nothing
on the floor except for carpet. The lava
lamp is bubbling on a shelf next to the
dresser, but the disco light is gone, as are
the plastic beads that used to hang from the
ceiling. I look at Livvy. "Who are you and
what have you done with my best friend?"

She laughs. "Mom made me promise to
clean it before you got here. I have never
worked so fast in my life."

"For me?" I say, fingertips pressed against
my chest.

Livvy does her Hollywood kiss-kiss thing again. "Only the best, dahling."

The room does seem ten times bigger.

"And do I detect a hint of lemony freshness?" I ask.

"This place could pass a military inspection," she says. "Just don't look under the bed."

"I won't," I say.

"Where do you want it?" Mr. Byer carries a TV with a built-in DVD/VCR. Livvy taps the top of her dresser. He puts the TV down.

"Wait," Livvy yells. She runs out of the room, then comes back carrying a small towel. "Don't want it to scratch," she says. She puts the towel over the top of her dresser, and Mr. Byer sets the TV on it.

"I'm leaving for the video store in ten minutes," he says. "Better decide what you want before I go."

I look at Livvy. She shrugs. "Horror? Comedy? Romance?" she asks.

"Romantic comedy?" I suggest.

Livvy nods. Then she grins.

"The Princess Bride," we say at the same

time. It is only our all-time favorite, and I haven't seen it in years. Okay, maybe months.

"Good choice," he says as he heads from the room.

"Thanks for the invite," I say. I toss my bag on the floor and sit down on Livvy's bed.

"Entirely my pleasure," she says. "Not entirely my idea, though."

"Huh?"

Livvy's cheeks blush a little. "Not that I wouldn't have wanted you to come, but it was really your mom's suggestion, after she saw what happened and all."

"Whatever," I say. "I appreciate it all the same."

Livvy sits down next to me. "Actually," she says, her voice lowered, "it wasn't all your mom's idea either."

I look at Livvy, not sure what she is talking about.

"After the Octopus ordeal, while you were dashing off to—wherever—Nate said something like 'That girl needs a break.'"

"You lie," I say, hoping she doesn't.

"Seriously," she says. "Next thing I

know, we get home from the fair, and your mom is calling my mom asking if it would be okay, and was I up for it."

"Your brother doesn't know I breathe air," I say.

"He doesn't think you're a toad."

The shimmy thing in my stomach makes me wonder if eating pizza is a good idea. I look Livvy straight in her brown eyes. She most definitely isn't lying.

Chapter 5

It's the middle of the night, and I have to go to the bathroom so bad that I think my eyeballs will pop out of my head from the pressure build-up. Livvy snores on the floor beside me. Seriously, she snores. And I haven't really been able to sleep since she told me her brother acknowledged that I'm not an amphibian.

There is no bathroom upstairs at Livvy's house except for the one in her parents' room, and I'm not about to go tiptoeing through their private space to use the facilities. I review my dilemma: the bathroom is downstairs, down a hallway, and past Nate's room. Nate is still awake. I know this

because I heard him come back from seeing
a movie and goofing off with Chris about 20
minutes ago. If I sneak downstairs to use the
bathroom, he'll know someone is up, and
he'll most likely come to investigate, which
means he will see me in all my middle-of-
the-night glory, which isn't very glorious. I
make a mental note to myself about not
drinking so much root beer before bedtime.

Livvy makes a snorkeling noise and rolls
over to the other side. My bladder begs me
to take the risk and avoid the pain. The
humiliation of wetting the bed seems
greater than the potential humiliation of
being caught looking gruesome in the middle of the night, so I slide on my leopard-
print slippers and venture down the stairs.

The necessary location is at the end of
the hallway. Nate's door is closed, but a
beam of light shoots out from under it. I
make my way to the bathroom and silently
shut the door. It's pitch-black and I grope
around for the light switch. The brightness
hurts my eyes, and all I really want is to get
back upstairs and try to get some sleep.

My business completed, I face a new set

of issues. How much noise will this make? What if Nate thinks it's Livvy? That might be good, because he'd probably ignore her. What if he thinks it's me and comes out of his room? On the surface, it might appear this is a good thing. A private, late-night conversation with the man I have fantasized about since I was old enough to fantasize? Sounds like a good option.

I imagine him, standing in his doorway, the outline of his body against the light coming from behind him. He motions to me, his deep voice whispers my name, calling me to come closer, closer. I lean forward, holding my breath, anticipating his touch—or dare I think it—his kiss. My heart pounds against my chest and I move even closer, until . . .

"Who's in the john?"

My eyes pop open and I turn, banging my knee against the cabinet. "Ow," I say, not meaning to blurt it so loud.

"Mattie?"

Blood rushes to my face. "Yeah, just a second." I flush the toilet and wash my hands, then splash cool water against my cheeks to keep them from looking so red. I turn off the light as I pull open the door. Maybe if I hurry, I can avoid looking into those perfect, brown eyes.

"You okay?" Nate says.

"Yeah," I say. I glance up.

Trapped. Those eyes are looking right into mine, and I'm sure he can see right into my heart. My face feels hot again, and I'm glad that the light in the hallway is so dim. "Sorry if I woke you." *Oh what a stunning conversationalist I am.*

"Nah, I was up."

Like I didn't notice, since I walked right past his door.

"How was your movie?" I say. I should be back in Livvy's room, but I somehow seem to be stuck here, in the hallway, by the bathroom.

"It was all right. Nothing to get excited about." Nate looks great. It's not fair. It's the middle of the night, and he should have to look as disgusting as I do.

"Well, goodnight," I say.

"Wait," he says. He puts his hand on my arm. I think my knees will melt and leave me in a puddle on the floor. His hand is warm. My heart beats like a hummingbird.

"You want a snack?" he asks.

I nod my head. It takes every ounce of concentration I have to make my head move up and down, because every other part of me wants to run screaming up the stairs to hide under the bed and giggle.

Nate moves his hand away, and I realize I've been holding my breath. He shuffles up the hallway toward the kitchen and I follow him. The house is making its nighttime noises, little creaking and groaning sounds that remind me how late it is and that I should be asleep. I notice the hum of the refrigerator and the clicking sound as the air conditioner switches off.

Nate takes two glasses from the cupboard and fills them with milk, then pulls out a bear-shaped bottle of honey and grabs a bag of dinner rolls. He hands one to me. "I love to drown these in honey," he says. He squeezes a long, glistening stream from the bear bottle, then takes a bite.

I drizzle little swirls on the top of my roll. "I'm usually a jelly person myself," I say. Nate laughs, then takes another bite.

"You excited to start high school?" he says, his mouth half-full.

I shrug. "It's just four more years of the same," I say. "I'm just looking forward to not having to spend every day with my brother."

"I dig your little brother. He's funny."

"Oh yeah, a laugh a minute," I say. "Try living with him, and then see how funny he is." This is not quite the direction I had imagined for our conversation, but I figure at least he's talking to me. This is a good thing.

"At least you won't ever have to go to school with him," Nate replies.

"You mean, like you have to go with Livvy?"

Nate stuffs the last bite of roll in his mouth, then takes a big drink of milk to wash it down. He nods. "Yeah, it's a drag."

A little zap of anger stings me, and I want to defend my best friend. But I also don't want to look like a complete dweeb in front of this guy. I mean, this is the first time he has really talked to me like I'm something other than a lower life form.

"She acts like a reject," Nate says. "It's embarrassing."

"Because she has a major crush on Chris?"

Nate groans. "It drives me up the wall. The ways she acts around him—sometimes I just want to shove her in a closet and lock it until she's forty or something."

I laugh. I can't help it. I'm nervous, so I wrap my hands around my glass of milk and try to get control.

"Sometimes I wish she was more like you," he says. His voice is soft now.

My heart starts the hummingbird thing again. In an effort to control my nerves, I grab my roll and tear little pieces from it.

"You're just so casual, you know? You don't make a big deal out of stuff like Livvy does."

My eyes focus on the growing pile of shredded roll. My fingers are sticky from the honey, and crumbs stick to them like I've been tarred and feathered. Honeyed and breaded.

Nate continues. "And you don't act like a geek around guys. You're really easy to talk to and stuff." He leans over the counter. I look up, and his face is so close to mine that I can smell the sweetness of the honey on his breath. Everything inside of me is twitching and shimmying, and I'm afraid I may lapse into convulsions if he gets any closer.

"What I mean," Nate says, his voice almost a whisper, "is that I like you, a lot."

My mouth freezes. My brain freezes. My eyes lock with his. He leans closer, and I can't believe it but his eyelids are lower and he gets closer, and I lean closer and I close my eyes, and before I know it, he kisses me and my insides feel like a million pieces of machinery flying apart all at once and melting into my toes.

And then it stops. I can't hear the house creaking or the refrigerator humming. All I can hear is the bird in my chest that flutters so hard I think it might beat itself to death. Nate steps back.

Blood rushes to my cheeks, down my neck, and I imagine that my skin is the color of strawberries. My lips feel warm. Part of me wants to run to Livvy, giggling and ready to gossip. Part of me wants to tackle

Nate and kiss his whole face. But I don't move—I can't move. I sit on the stool at the Byers' kitchen counter, my fingers covered with honey and crumbs. I wonder if this is what someone feels just before they go into shock. Maybe this is shock?

"Are you okay?" Nate's head is tipped to one side like a puppy. *Like Donny*, I think. I force the image of my little brother out of my head. He isn't going to ruin this moment for me.

"Yeah," I manage to say.

"You looked like you might be sick or something."

A little laugh escapes from me, and my body feels lighter somehow. "No, I'm okay."

Nate looks relieved. He steps around the counter and sits on the stool next to me.

"Cause for a minute there, I thought maybe you were totally disgusted."

"No, it's okay. It was great." I wonder what time it is, then I decide I don't care. I hope time stops completely and lets me sit here forever.

"Good," he says, "cause I might want to do it again."

I turn my head to look at him, partly because I don't believe him and partly to make it easier, just in case. He looks right at me, and I lower my gaze so I don't seem too obvious, too eager. He cups my chin in his hand and lifts my head so I look right into his eyes again.

"Is that okay? If I kiss you again?"

"Uh-huh," is all I can manage to say. I close my eyes—waiting—hoping it will be just as good the second time. His hand moves away from my chin. I wait to feel his lips brush against mine. The fluttering inside my chest has picked up again and I can't remember if I brushed my teeth, so I hold my breath so that I don't somehow breathe bad breath on him.

But nothing happens.

I open one eye. Nate is looking at me, smiling. I would like to crawl under the stool and die of embarrassment now. Blood races through my face again, all the way to my scalp. I turn away and sweep the pile of crumbs that used to be my roll into my hands. I move to the cupboard where the trashcan is and brush the crumbs off, then

go to the sink to wash off the honey. I look
for a dish towel to dry my hands, and I try to
avoid looking at Nate. What a twit I am. As
I turn from the sink, I run right into him.

"Sorry," he says. He puts his hands on
my shoulders, and I think I might turn to
mush. "I didn't mean to make you uncomfortable."

"I'm not," I say, a little too loud. "I
mean, no big deal."

I look up into his face, and he leans over
and kisses me again. It feels like a bolt of
lightning hits me between the eyes. He
smiles, turns, and heads down the hall
toward his room. I lean back against the
sink, partly for balance, partly because I
don't know what else to do. "That was
weird," I say to no one.

Back in Livvy's room, I lie on the floor
and review these events. My first kiss.
Okay, not my *first* kiss, but my first *real* kiss.
That thing with Josh Hill in fifth grade
shouldn't count. Especially since it was a
dare, and while he won the two-pound bag
of candy, he didn't bother sharing any of
them with me. But this time . . . this was

an "oh-my-gosh-I-can't-believe-it's-really-happening" kiss. A kiss that can make your innards feel like you're in the middle of a nuclear meltdown—that kind of kiss has to count.

Maybe I should wake up Livvy and tell her. A twinge of guilt goes through me. I didn't defend my friend. I should have told Nate that Livvy is *not* a geek, that she is one of the coolest, funniest people I know. But if I did that, he probably wouldn't have kissed me. And if I tell Livvy what happened, she'd probably say something to him, probably in front of their parents, and then my chances of him kissing me again would be, like, none. Better to keep my little piece of heaven than to run the risk of causing family turmoil.

Chapter 6

Yet Another Pop Quiz

Yes, it's you again, as me. You awaken the morning after your first real kiss, still in the home of the man of your dreams who provided you with said kiss. Oh, and his sister, also your best friend. After the necessary morning rituals of brushing your teeth, combing your hair, and putting on clothes more appropriate than the tee-shirt you slept in, you and your best friend make your way to the breakfast table. The man of your dreams sits at the counter and greets you by saying, "Are you still here?" You respond by:

    A. smiling, batting your eyes, and let-
        ting him know that you understand
        he is only trying to deal with his
        family in a way that won't let on to
        your shared secret;

    B. gasping and showing that you are
        deeply wounded by his hurtful
        remarks; or,

    C. saying, "And a pleasant good morn-
        ing to you, too, butthead."

That final response comes from Livvy.
The best I manage to come up with is pretending to ignore Nate, something that I'm
not very good at. In all the times I've been
at Livvy's house, I haven't ever felt uncomfortable. Until now. It's like pulling on a
favorite shirt and realizing it's too small.
There is this awkward moment where you
think, "This can't be right," but you come to
realize that—yes—something is definitely
wrong here.

Mrs. Byer brings a plate of toast to the
table. "Would you girls like some melon?"
she asks. She puts a bowl on the table that
is filled with chunks of cantaloupe, water-

melon, and honeydew. I grab the big spoon
from the bowl and begin dishing fruit onto
a plate. Livvy takes only a few pieces of the
watermelon, then reaches for the toast.

"Where's the honey?" she asks.

My stomach does a little flip as I think
about the bear-shaped bottle. A hundred
images flash through my mind. I look up at
Nate—I can't help it. He looks at me and
winks, and my stomach flips again.
Suddenly, I can't think about melon. All I
can think about is the taste of honey and
the softness of Nate's lips against mine.

"Do you want to go to the rec center
and go swimming?" Livvy shoves a piece of
watermelon in her mouth. Nate walks past
us. I want to follow him, see where he's
going or what he's doing, but I keep my butt
firmly planted. I don't even turn my head.

"Swimming sounds good," I say. "I just
need to check with my mom and dad and
make sure it's okay."

Livvy hands me the phone and I dial.

"That should be all right," Mom says.
"But I want you . . ." She doesn't need to
finish. I know what's coming.

" . . . to take your brother." I say it in unison with her. "Thanks a lot, Mom."

There is noise in the background, and I hear Donny barking. Mom tells him he can go swimming with me if he finishes his breakfast and gets dressed. Donny makes even more noise. I roll my eyes and sigh.

"What time are you going?" Mom asks.

I look at Livvy. "What time?"

Livvy looks at her mom. "What time can we go?"

Mrs. Byer looks at her watch. "How about noon?" She looks at me. "Tell your mom we'll bring you home to get your things."

"My things include my brother. Is that okay?" I'm hoping she'll say no.

"That's fine," she says, as if I'd told her I was bringing my sunscreen and not Donny Disaster.

"Noon," I say to Mom.

Mrs. Byer drives us to my house. To my great disappointment, Nate is not with us. He stayed home to work on the Mazda.

I climb out of the minivan. "Be right back." It's quiet inside, and I silently pray that maybe Donny is taking a nap and

won't be able to come with us. With my
swim things stuffed in a canvas bag, I head
for the door. Mom is in the kitchen, lying
in wait for me.

"Haven't you forgotten something?"
she says.

"Sunblock," I say. "I'll borrow some from
Livvy."

Mom shakes her head. She isn't smiling.
"Nice try."

"Mom," I say with my best disgruntled
whine.

"Mattie," she says with her best *I'm
warning you* tone.

The door to the den flies open, and
Donny comes bounding into the kitchen,
the shiny red collar around his neck. He
sits up and begs, then tips his head to one
side and looks at me. It reminds me of Nate
looking at me after that kiss. *That kiss*, I
think, and my knees get wobbly again.

Mom clips the leash to Donny's collar
and holds it out for me.

"No way," I say. I look at Donny. "Dogs
aren't allowed in the pool."

He whimpers and looks up at Mom.

"Just ignore her," she says, then she fixes me with a look that says she means business. "You keep an eye on him. I don't want you off flirting with the lifeguard and ignoring your brother."

"I won't be flirting with anyone," I say. *Unless Nate shows up.*

Mom reaches into her pocket and hands me ten dollars. "This isn't just for you and Olivia."

"Okay," I say.

"Make sure your brother gets a snack and something to drink."

"I get it. You don't have to make it a federal case."

I take the money and stuff it in the bag with my suit. Then I take the leash from her hand and turn to go. Donny gets up from all fours and starts walking. It surprises me, but it doesn't make me less bugged about taking him along.

Mrs. Byer is rummaging in her purse for something as we hop into the car. Livvy smiles at Donny and he giggles. "All buckled?" asks Mrs. Byer as she pulls onto the street.

"Arf," says Donny.

Mrs. Byer looks at me in the rearview mirror.

"It's a long story," I say.

"How's my favorite doggy dude?" Livvy says.

Donny starts to pant. "Arf, arf."

"Hey," Livvy says, "you never told me what happened with the whole spike thing."

"I was sure my mom would flip a widget, but she thought it was great." I sigh. "She made my dad get video shots of him modeling his spikes."

"Arf, arf," Donny says.

"You looked awesome," Livvy says.

Donny smiles at her.

The pool is crowded for a Sunday afternoon. Everyone is trying to squeeze the last little bit out of summer they can.

Livvy finds a lounge chair and tosses her stuff on it. "Looks like we'll have to share," she says.

I unclip Donny's leash and toss it on the ground. Donny sticks his head into his bag and, with his teeth, pulls out his water wings.

"Right on," Livvy says. "Doggy flotation

devices." She blows up the water wings and helps Donny slip his arms into them.

"No running," I say. Donny tips his head and looks at me like he is surprised I knew that's what he was thinking. He walks with exaggerated slowness to the steps of the shallow end, then watches me as I watch him get into the water. Livvy and I follow, hanging out on the steps to get maximum amplification of the sun. Little kids splash around us, squealing and laughing. Donny is dog paddling, of course. The sunlight shatters into millions of sparkles on the water, and I have to shade my eyes to keep from being blinded.

"You want to go to the mall this week?" Livvy asks.

"Depends on the day." I lean back on my elbows and close my eyes. "When Mom gets her work schedule, I'll let you know what days I've got Donny Duty."

"That's the only part of having a little brother that would suck."

I laugh—well, snort actually. "That's not the only part that sucks."

"I don't know why you rag on him so

much. He's, like, a ten on the adorable scale."

"You'd think that for about five minutes if you lived with him." I shade my face with my hand and look at Livvy. "Between him and my parents, it's like living on some demented sitcom."

"Yeah, well, it's better than living in the freak show at my house."

"You want to compare?" I say. "Okay, when your brother's friends come over, you at least get decent eye candy. When Donny's friends come over, I get to watch Elmo and hope no one spills their juice."

"I'd take Elmo and juice over hearing 'Hey Nate, I didn't know you had a little brother. Oh, dude. That's your sister? Sorry man..'" Livvy makes her voice low and husky.

"Okay, how about waking up to having your face licked at 5:30 in the morning?"

"How about taking cold showers every morning because your jerk-face brother uses all the hot water?"

"Oh, let's talk about having to watch Disney Channel for hours on end because your brother won't let you change the chan-nel without screaming."

Livvy sits up straight. "How about having to listen every Sunday to every stat on every football player that's playing that day."

"How about having your brother drag your favorite pair of slippers into the yard and burying them." My chest feels like there's a belt inside that's cinching tighter and tighter.

"No, how about your brother dragging *you* outside, tying you up to the mailbox in your pajamas while playing 'alien invasion' with his friends."

"No way," I say.

Livvy isn't laughing. She looks at me. No, she glares at me. "Seriously," she says. "It was totally humiliating."

"If I did anything like that to Donny, my parents would never let me see the light of day again."

"Yeah, well, that's another difference." Livvy leans back again. "My parents thought that it was hysterical. They told everyone about how funny it was."

I lean back, too. "My dad gets everything on video so it will survive for all eternity and maybe win him ten grand on

'America's Funniest Home Videos.'"

The hot sun relaxes me, and I feel like taking a nap. I'm hoping to pick up just a smidge more tan to make up for not having enough time in the sun this summer. The cinching feeling comes back. So many things slipped past me this summer because of watching Donny. Because of Mom working.

At first I thought it would be cool to have Mom work at the bakery. "Just three days a week," she said. "You won't even notice I'm gone." And the hours sounded great. She would start at 5:00 in the morning and get home by 2:00 in the afternoon. Dad doesn't leave for the insurance office until 9:00, so we all figured that five hours wasn't that big of a deal.

Of course, I hadn't figured on what it would be like to spend all day with Donny. By 2:00, I'm totally wiped. And Mom always has to stay late or run errands on the way home, so my day is completely shot by the time she comes home to relieve me.

Somewhere around the middle of July, I made the decision that I would never have kids. They are too much work, too time consuming, and they leave you with no life of your own.

It occurs to me, as I'm thinking of how Donny has cured me of ever having a family, that I can't hear him splashing and barking. I sit up straight, shade my eyes, and look around. I can't see him.

"Livvy," I say as I stand up. "I can't see Donny." Livvy bolts to a standing position and starts scanning the pool.

The water shoots the sunlight right into my eyes despite my efforts to block it. I squint into the bright glare. "Donny," I call. I wade into the shallow water and keep searching. "Donny."

"Bark."

I turn toward the sound of my brother. He's walking along the edge of the pool—by the deep end.

"What are you doing?" I ask. That's a mistake. Donny takes off running. He's heading for the diving board.

"Donny, no," I yell. As he rounds the corner to get in line to jump off the board, his feet slip and I watch in horror-movie-slow-motion as he tumbles and falls into the pool. Livvy is out of the water and running. I swim, pushing hard against the water, shoving people out of my way. I see Donny's frightened face as he sinks down. I dive under and kick toward him. The sounds become muffled and distorted. Donny's eyes are wide. I kick hard, my ears popping as I go deeper, then I reach and grab his arm, pulling him to me. I push with my free arm until we reach the surface. Everything immediately becomes sharp and loud.

Donny coughs and sputters, water spewing from his mouth. Breathing hard, I reach for the edge of the pool, my heart pounding furiously against my chest wall. A lifeguard drags Donny out and onto the cement. I can only cling to the edge of the pool, sucking in deep breaths of air. A tremor runs through my whole body.

"Mattie," Livvy says. She offers me a hand, but I heave myself from the water and sit on the pavement, my head between my knees.

Donny cries and I lift my head to see what's happening. The lifeguard kneels over him, blocking my view.

"Donny," I say, moving closer.

The lifeguard helps him sit up. "Where's your mother?" he asks.

"At home," I say.

The lifeguard looks at me like he doesn't trust me. "Who's responsible for him?"

"I am," I say. "I'm his sister. Is he okay?"

Donny rubs at his eyes. His crying subsides to a whimper.

"He'll be fine. Just swallowed some water. Might have bumped his head, but nothing serious." He walks back to the white lifeguard chair that oversees the pool.

Anger threads through my veins. "I told you not to run. This is what happens when you don't listen." I stand, my shadow falling across his body. Donny starts to cry again. He pulls his knees up and won't look at me.

"I'll bet you got scared," Livvy says in a quiet voice. She moves next to Donny and rubs his back. I want to push her out of the way and tell her to mind her own business. Donny pulls away and holds his arms up for me.

"I'm not picking you up," I say, keeping

my voice flat. Adrenaline continues to surge through my veins.

"Come here," Livvy says. She holds her arms out, and Donny lets her lift him.

Now I'm really angry. "Don't baby him," I say. "It's his own stupid fault that he fell. If he'd listened when I told him not to run, he wouldn't have gotten hurt."

Livvy looks at me like I've suddenly turned orange. "Back off," she says. "He didn't mean to get hurt. It's not like he did it to tick you off."

Why is she defending him?

Donny coughs again, then rests his head on Livvy's shoulder. "Let's go sit down for a minute," Livvy says. She carries him to the lounge chair. He holds on to her, then, when I am looking right at him, he sticks his tongue out at me.

Chapter 7

At first I think I won't tell Mom and Dad about the episode at the pool. After all, no harm, no foul. I can just tell them we had a great time, no big deal. Then I realize there is no guarantee that Donny won't say anything, and if I tell him not to, that will guarantee he blabs the whole thing the minute we get home. I also figure that either Mrs. Byer or Livvy will ask how Donny is doing at some point down the road, and I'll have to go through and explain the whole thing to my mom. Not only would I be in trouble for the initial near-drowning event, but also for not letting Mom know immediately after it happened. The punishment would be compounded.

I'm not a good liar. I'm not good at even thinking about being a good liar.

Dad is in the backyard barbequing, and Mom is boiling corn on the cob on the stove. Donny drops his swim stuff on the floor and runs upstairs to his room. The house feels like it's 112 degrees inside.

"We're having a picnic on the patio," Mom says. "It's cooler in the shade."

"It's cooler in Death Valley," I say.

Mom rubs her forehead with the back of her hand, but she doesn't respond. I take that as a good sign and decide to fess up about the pool incident.

"Um, Donny will probably say something about this later, so I may as well tell you now."

Mom turns to look at me. "What's wrong?" she asks in that "worst-case scenario" tone.

"It's nothing. It's no big deal. It's just that Donny was horsing around, and he slipped and fell into the pool. He's fine. He just got scared and swallowed some water."

"How did *that* happen?" Mom folds her arms and looks me right between the eyes.

"It wasn't my fault. He took off running, and when I told him to stop, he didn't."

She holds my stare. "And where were you?"

"In the pool," I say. "He took off for the deep end. I told him 'no,' but he didn't stop."

"And how did he get out of the pool without you noticing?"

"It was busy. There were a lot of kids. I closed my eyes for, like, I don't know, two seconds maybe."

"That's all it takes with a four-year-old."

"He's fine, Mom. Not a big deal. I just didn't want you to freak out, okay?"

"I'm not freaked out, I'm concerned."

Her words sting and I lash back. "I spent my whole summer watching this kid while you were at work and wherever, and he seems to have lived through it just fine, and *now* you're concerned?" I turn to go up to my room.

"Mattie, I'm not finished." Mom's voice has a sharp edge.

I stop walking but stay facing the hall-

way. "What?" I wonder if I have made a
huge mistake telling her the truth.

"Look at me when I'm talking to you."

I turn and face her. My jaw clenches.

"I'm sorry you feel that your whole summer has been imposed upon by watching
your brother a few days a week." She steps
away from the stove, her arms still folded
tightly against her middle. "If we hadn't
needed the money, I wouldn't have taken the
job. But I see now that you resent this extra
responsibility."

"Mom," I start, but she interrupts me.

"If this resentment is going to cause you
to be irresponsible, I'll find other arrange-
ments. It's not worth putting your brother
in danger because you can't stay focused on
caring for him."

I suddenly understand what it means
when people say their blood boiled with
anger. Every inch of me feels hot—boiling
hot. I am Vesuvius erupting, I am so hot.

"I'm not his mother," I say so loudly that
it hurts my ears. "It's not my job to be
responsible for him, it's yours. But you
don't seem to care, because you have me as

the built-in nanny. Heaven forbid I do any-thing for myself and exclude him, because it might interfere with whatever plans you have that are so amazingly important. I took him with me today, even though you weren't working. He got to ride with me at the amusement park, even though he was too little." Words spill out like lava, and I draw in a long breath.

"You don't care how I'm feeling, you don't care about my life, you don't care about me, as long as Donny the Wonder Dog is happy and you can do whatever it is you want to do. You probably didn't even think about the fact I might want to have a life other than my brother. Well, I do." I didn't realize I had swallowed those words down for so long, and now that they are out, I feel relieved.

Mom's voice comes softer than I expect and catches me off-guard. "That's enough," she says. "It wasn't my choice to go back to work, but it was better than having to sell our house or cut back on other things like food and clothing." She lets out a long sigh. "I found a job I thought we could all work

with, so that Donny didn't have to go to
daycare. So that the money I made could be
used for our family."

The whole money thing hadn't really
been discussed with me. I had heard Mom
and Dad talking about the budget, especially after Dad quit his old job and started his
new insurance agency. But I thought things
were okay, financially speaking. I thought
Mom took the job as a way to get a break
from "Barney" and "Sesame Street," not to
make sure we had enough money.

"Nobody bothered to tell me about any of
this," I say. "It would have been nice to know
that's what was going on, instead of you and
Dad just assuming I would get it." Anger
pounds in my heart like a hammer.

"I guess I thought you understood. I'm
sorry. I should have talked through this better with you."

Her words don't really comfort me. I
still feel like I've been a convenience. Like
a 7-11 store. "It was just easier to ditch
Donny with me than to explain what was
going on, I guess."

Mom wipes at her eyes. I can't stand to

see her cry, even if I think I'm right.

"Mom, I'm sorry. Look, I didn't mean . . ."

"This has been a—challenging time," she says. "Challenging for all of us. We've all had to make some sacrifices. I guess I just didn't want to see how much I was really asking you to give up." She draws a deep breath and lets it out slow. "I rely on you so much, I guess I didn't want to think that it was a burden on you."

"It's okay," I say. "I mean, it's not all okay, but . . ."

"Mattie, we'll work something out for this coming week. You won't have to watch him."

Suddenly I'm very confused. I want to shout "Right on," but there is something about Mom's voice. She really needs me. Really needs my help.

"I can watch him this week. It's okay."

"I'll figure something out so you can have the week off to get ready for school."

I don't know what to say. Confusion feels like a worm in my head, weaving around in my brain and muddling my thoughts.

"Tell me again, what happened at the pool," Mom says. She turns to the stove and takes the pan of corn off the burner. Her sudden change in subject matter feels like an electric jolt. I snap my attention to the pool, steer the worm to remember what happened.

"He was running. He slipped and fell, landed in the deep end of the pool. The lifeguard checked him out and said he was okay. He swallowed a little water is all."

"Did he have his water wings on?" she asks.

"Yeah," I say. "But the lifeguard says those things are worthless. They're really more for a parent's peace of mind than any kind of safety thing." My words don't sound like my own. It's like my head is underwater again. I'm still trying to figure out what just happened, why I made Mom cry and why she switched gears like this.

Mom nods. "Did the lifeguard have to pull him out of the water?"

"No," I say. "I got him out." I try to sound very low-key. I don't want to upset my mom any more.

"I'm glad you were there, then."

I scramble to find something that will ease her mind. "If it had been a big deal, we would have come right home. Donny wanted to stay and 'fwim.'" I use Donny's word. This gets a small laugh.

"Go tell your brother to get ready for dinner. This corn is done, and I think the chicken should be about ready."

I toss my wet stuff in the laundry room, then head upstairs. I feel off balance, almost dizzy. "Dinner is ready," I call as I pass Donny's door. He's playing cars on his rug and looks up at me.

"When we go fwim again?" Donny says.

When pigs sprout wings, I think. "I don't know," I say. "I got in big trouble because you fell in the pool."

"Why you get in twuhbo?"

"Because it scares Mom to think you might get hurt, and it would be my fault if something bad happened while I was watching you."

Donny looks confused.

"Never mind," I say. "Dinner is ready, so pick your cars up and let's go eat." Donny runs downstairs, leaving his cars exactly where they are.

Nothing is said at dinner about Donny falling in the pool. Not even Donny says anything about it. By 8:30, I've almost let go of the whole event. Then Livvy calls.

"So, chica, did your mom kill you? Threaten to kill you? Take away your birthday?"

"You sound like you want me to be in trouble," I say.

"No," Livvy says. "I just want to know how bad the damage is, so I'll know if we can go to the mall this week."

"What's at the mall that you are dying to go see?"

"Chris got a job at Music Depot. I think I need a few new CDs."

I laugh. "You're a toad, remember?"

"Thanks for that reminder," she says. "But Nate offered to drive us."

My stomach does a flip-flop thing that makes me wish I hadn't opted for the third piece of chicken. That kiss.

"Hello?"

"Sorry," I say. "I was looking at my CDs

and wondering what I need to add to my collection."

"Liar," Livvy says.

"Not."

"Oh, you so are. You were drooling over the prospect of riding in the Mazda with my brother."

If you only knew. "Am not."

"Are too, chica, but whatever. So when can you go?"

"Mom gets her new work schedule tomorrow. I'll let you know when she gets home from work."

"Deal," she says. "Call me tomorrow as soon as you know."

I spend the rest of the evening laying on my bed, remembering that kiss. I wonder if I'll ever get that chance again. I wonder if it will be as exciting as the first time. I wonder if Nate will ask me out. I wonder myself to sleep.

* * *

"Wake up, Sleeping Beauty."

I open my eyes. Dad sits on the edge of my bed. "I have to go to my office, so I need you to get up and watch your brother for an hour or two."

"Mom said I could have the week off."

"I know," Dad says. "I'm sorry. I thought I could hang out here today, but something came up."

"What time is it?"

Dad looks at his watch. "10:00."

"Why did you let me sleep so late?" My internal alarm usually wakes me up by 7:00. School-year conditioning.

"I thought you needed the extra rest. Besides," he says as he stands to leave, "it's one of the last days you have left to sleep in. I thought I'd let you enjoy it."

"But shouldn't you have been to work an hour ago?"

Dad stops just inside the door. "That's one of the benefits of owning your own business." He smiles. "I need to use that benefit more often, don't you think?"

I nod.

Donny watches a Barney video. I make a bowl of cereal and slide into a chair at the kitchen table. Donny coughs.

After breakfast I finish the laundry.

Normally I'm just supposed to fold the clothes, but after yesterday I do an extra load to help out Mom. At noon, I fix ham and cheese sandwiches for me and Donny. He sits at the table and pulls the cheese off the bread. He didn't even ask me to cut it up and put it in the dog bowl.

The phone rings and before I answer it, I know it's Mom. She calls at noon every day she has to work.

"How are things at the house?"

"Same as it ever was," I say. "Donny's not eating his lunch." In the background I can hear the noise of the bakery, customers asking for chocolate chip cookies and wondering when the French bread will be out of the oven.

"I'm only working on Wednesday this week," Mom says. "I asked them for a few less hours."

"Oh," I say, not sure exactly how I should respond to this. "Is that going to be okay?"

"I think so," Mom says. "I've really got to figure out what I'm going to do when you go to school next week." The Queen of Procrastination strikes again.

"Um, yeah, that would be important."

"I've got to get back to work now. I'll see you about 2:00."

"Bye, Mom."

Donny has pulled the ham off his sandwich now. He's poking his finger in it and making little holes. Swiss ham.

"Don't play with it, eat it," I say.

"I firsty," he says. I pour him some apple juice. He takes a few bites of ham, then pushes his plate aside.

"You need to finish your lunch."

"I full."

"How can you be full? You hardly ate anything."

"I full."

I take his plate and empty it, then rinse it off and stick it in the dishwasher. "You want to go outside and ride your bike?"

He shakes his head.

"Play soccer?"

He shakes his head.

"So what do you want to do?"

Donny goes upstairs, then returns with the leash.

"And what do you want me to do with

that?" I ask.

"Go to Livvy houf."

"Not today, Donny." I brace for crying or a fight. Instead Donny drops the leash and heads back to the TV. He flops onto the sofa and rests his head on a pillow.

Mom comes in at 2:15. I'm stunned.

"You're home on time," I say. "What's the occasion?"

"I left a few minutes early. No big deal." She grabs a can of soda from the fridge and pops it open. "Where's your brother?"

"Sleeping."

Mom looks at the clock on the microwave. "What time did he go down for his nap?"

"About 12:30 he fell asleep on the couch. He woke up about 1:00, and I took him upstairs."

Mom's brow furrows. "Did you take his temperature?"

"No," I say, confused by her question.

"Did he feel hot?"

"Well, considering it's about a hundred and ten in this house, I guess yeah, he probably felt hot."

Mom looks like she wants to say something about my attitude, but she doesn't. Instead she goes up the stairs to the bathroom and gets the electronic thermometer from the medicine cabinet. I follow behind her, wondering what is going on, wondering if I missed something important that I should have known about.

She moves toward Donny's room, opens the door, and steps inside. Donny is asleep on his bed, clutching his favorite blanket. His face is damp and flushed pink, like he's been playing in the sun too long. But he hasn't. He's barely moved from the sofa all day.

Mom takes his temperature. He doesn't move. She heads back to the bathroom.

"One hundred point one," she says.

"Is that bad?"

"Not necessarily. He could just have another cold." Mom puts the thermometer away.

"I thought he'd gotten over that," I say.

She leaves the bathroom and I follow her downstairs again. "I'll just let him sleep and see how he feels when he wakes up."

Chapter 8

A Very Short Pop Quiz

Do you believe in miracles?

    A. yes

    B. no

My answer is A. And they happen on Tuesdays. I know this because it is Tuesday night, and my day has been filled with miracles. Three of them, to be exact.

The first miracle happened this morning. I got to sleep in again. That's two days in a row for those of you keeping score at home. No Donny bouncing on my bed, licking my face. No Mom or Dad waking me up to say I need to watch my brother. My eyeballs didn't see daylight until 9:30 in the morning.

The second miracle occurred shortly after the first. Livvy called.

"Can we go today?"

"To the mall?"

"No, to the moon. Duh. What have we been talking about for the past few days?"

Not only did my mom agree, but my dad slipped me an extra fifty bucks. Yes, you read that right. Fifty dollars to spend. On me. At the mall. This after the raging fit about money I got from my mom just two days before. Maybe it was a guilt thing. Maybe it was a payoff for all the free babysitting I've done. Who knows? Who cares? I got the extra cash and I wasn't about to look that gift horse in the mouth, or any other place.

The third miracle happened at the mall. Now, I don't typically picture the mall as a miraculous sort of location. In fact, I'd say it's pretty much the least miraculous place I can think of, except for maybe the dentist's office.

Livvy and I cruised the stores for those last-minute back-to-school bargains. Nate

disappeared into the Music Depot to harass
Chris. Livvy and I made our way over after
a respectable wait. As I flipped through the
new CDs looking for something to grab my
attention, someone grabbed me from
behind. I about jumped over the CD rack
and left my skin behind.

"Hey," Nate said. His warm hand rested
on my hip.

Once I got my heart rate down below a
thousand, I answered him. "Hey."

"There's a 'welcome back' stomp at
school on Friday night."

I looked around for Livvy to see if she
was catching any of this. She stood at the
counter, looking at gift cards and discount
stuff while Chris helped customers. I looked
at Nate. "Yeah," I managed to say. *Such
stunning repartee.*

He moved next to me and started casual-
ly flipping through CDs that I doubt he has
any interest in. "So, I wonder," he said, his
voice soft and yummy to my ears. "Maybe
you'd like to go with me."

My heart rate jumped back up to hummingbird speed. My brain spun so fast I

thought I'd wind up with cerebral damage. "Um, yeah. Sure," I said, trying to sound calmer than my body functions wanted to allow.

"Great," Nate said. He touched my arm and a jolt raced through me, hitting every extremity at warp speed. "I'll call you later with details."

Then he walked away.

It is a good thing that the racks in the Music Depot are bolted to the floor, because I felt like I might fall over and take the whole Hip Hop section with me. Three miracles in less than eight hours. That has to be some sort of record. I wonder who I call at Guinness to verify this. Does Guinness have a world record for miracles?

The rest of my day is a blur. I spent most of the fifty dollars, but not all of it. I ate something at the food court, but I don't remember what. I talked to Livvy about stuff, none of which I can recall.

Now, I'm waiting for the phone to ring. Waiting to work out those oh-so-important details about my first date with Nate. My first date. Okay, my first *real* date. That thing with Josh Crowe at the junior high science fair shouldn't count. Especially since my science project was better than his and, oh, never mind.

Ring, dang it, ring.

Obviously sheer will power isn't working. I wonder if I should call him. I could call and ask for Livvy, and then ask if I can—no, that won't work because I never did tell her that her brother asked me out. Can you say dilemma?

I vaguely recall Livvy saying something during lunch about the stomp. I vaguely recall me saying something about going with her. Nate was still at the Music Depot bugging Chris.

Yikes.

"Mattie," my mom says. "Are you in there?"

"Yeah," I answer.

"Livvy's on the phone for you."

Great. "Got it." I didn't hear it ring.

"So what's up?" Livvy asks.

My heart thumps a little harder. "Nothing. What's up with you?" I'm hoping that's what she expected to hear. I try to sound normal, but nothing is normal right now.

"A little birdie told me you have a date this Friday."

Busted. "Um . . ." I force my brain to find the right words. I don't know how I'm supposed to deal with this.

"Why didn't you tell me at lunch?" Livvy's voice is flat. She sounds royally ticked off.

"Shock," I say.

"Very funny." She doesn't sound amused.

"Seriously." I'm going for the honest approach. I really wish I were a good liar. "It was a huge surprise to me, and I didn't know what to say. In fact, I barely remember talking to you during lunch. I barely remember eating lunch, I was that stunned."

"Yeah, well, have a great time. I'll see you on Monday."

With that, the line goes dead. *Hello, Guinness? Cancel that last call about record-setting miracles.*

Now what? Do I call back and try to explain things? Do I call back and tell her what a booger she's being? Do I ignore the whole thing and hope it will go away? The thing is, I've never been in a situation that required asking these kinds of questions before, and I don't want to make the wrong choice. This is *so* not fun.

I decide I should call back and try to explain.

Nate answers and my brain instantly turns to mush. "Uh, hi, um, Nate. This is Mattie."

"Hey, what's up?"

"Can I talk to Livvy?"

"Don't you want to talk to me?"

More than I want to keep breathing. "Well, yeah, I do, but I need to talk to Livvy."

Nate covers the phone and yells. I hear muffled voices. "Livvy says to tell you she's not here."

That feels like a blow to my gut. I sit in stunned silence for a moment.

"I guess now you have to talk to me," Nate says in his yummy voice, only it's not sounding so yummy right now, because I really want to talk to my best friend. I really want a chance to explain things to her.

"I thought maybe I could pick you up about 7:00, and we could grab something to eat?"

I'm too distracted to really concentrate on what he's saying. "Yeah, okay."

"Great. So I'll see you Friday at 7:00, unless you can come by sometime this week to visit."

"Depends," I say.

"On what?"

"On whether Livvy will let me in the house or not."

He chuckles like this is some sort of joke. "Don't worry about her. She's just jealous."

But I am worried about her. "Will you ask her to call me?"

"I'll ask," he says, then he pauses. I can hear a television in the background. "I don't know if she'll answer, but I'll definitely ask."

I hang up the phone and sit on the edge of my bed, wondering if what I did was wrong. Livvy has known forever that I had it big for her brother. I thought she would be happy for me. I thought, being that she's my best friend and all, she would be excited. Her not being excited makes me mad. *What kind of a friend does that to you?*

Maybe Tuesdays aren't as miraculous as I thought.

Chapter 9

Wednesdays are not miraculous at all. Mom left for work hours ago, and despite his promise to stay with Donny, Dad says he has to go to his office for some paperwork.

Donny watches a Disney show, curled up on the sofa. He sniffles a little now and then, but otherwise he keeps very quiet. I kind of like that he doesn't drive me insane asking for toys or snacks or another movie. I play a few computer games, and I read *Cosmo Girl* straight through with no interruptions.

On the other hand, this makes me nervous. Donny is never dull. Not ever.

After I finish *Cosmo Girl*, I go check on

him. He's watching 'Liddow Moomaid' for the bazillionth time. But he's not singing 'Undoo the Fea.' He's not pretending to be the crab. He's not dancing. He's not Donny. I'm worried.

At noon, when Mom calls to check in, I try not to sound worried. When she asks how Donny is, though, I tell her anyway. Darn that not lying thing.

"Something's wrong," I say. "He's just laying around, doing nothing."

Mom is quiet for a moment. "I'll call and see if I can take him to the pediatrician when I get home." There is a lot of noise in the bakery. "Just keep an eye on him and call me if he seems to be getting worse."

I agree to call if he gets worse, though I'm not sure what worse would look like. This is the worst I've ever seen him. Except for maybe the time he got into Mom's makeup and covered himself in Ivory Bisque #3 by Max Factor. Even that was sort of cute. I find nothing cute about the lump on the sofa.

***

Mom makes it home from work by 2:10, and I wonder if she set some sort of land-speed record. She throws her purse and keys on the counter and immediately starts looking for Donny.

I've taken over the spot on the sofa where Donny spent most of the day. "He's sleeping in his bed," I say. "I carried him upstairs about twenty minutes ago."

"I've got an appointment with the pediatrician at 4:00," Mom says. "I'll let him sleep until it's time to go."

"He's still in his jammies. He didn't want to get dressed."

Mom takes a seat on the sofa next to me. Her eyes look tired. She still has on her hair net from the bakery. "I'm sure this is just some sort of bug he's picked up."

"Probably," I say.

She pulls the hair net off and balls it up in her hands. "I'll go check on him."

The phone rings. It might be Livvy, so I leap off the sofa and dash for the cordless.

"Hey, beautiful."

It takes me a moment to figure out that the voice belongs to Nate. I get caught off-guard at being called "beautiful" because only my dad ever says that to me.

"Hey," I say. I'm waiting for my knees to start their melting thing. It's a little slow showing up, but eventually I notice that weird sensation like my legs might crumple.

"We're still on for Friday, right?"

"Um, yeah," I say. I can't believe it, but I had almost forgotten he asked me.

"That wasn't a very energetic answer," Nate says. His voice registers something between teasing and hurt.

"Oh," I say. "Sorry. I've spent all day taking care of Donny. He's pretty sick, so I'm a little distracted."

"Sorry to hear that," Nate says, sounding a little more relaxed. "Hey, can you get out for a movie tonight?"

My knees are really wobbly now. "Like a date?" I say. *Yet another stunning example of my wit and charm.*

Nate chuckles. "Yeah, like a date."

"I don't know. I have to ask. Is Livvy going?"

There is a pause, then Nate lets out a long breath. "Does she have to?"

My parents had the big "dating lecture" with me for my fourteenth birthday. Not that it was necessary then. But the basic rule is that, until I'm sixteen, groups are the only acceptable form of dating.

"I think so," I say. "But if you invite Chris, it won't be a problem."

"Yeah, it would be a big problem," Nate says. Now he sounds amused, which confuses me.

"Why so?"

"Because I think his girlfriend would object to him going out with my dorky little sister."

"Girlfriend?" I blurt, sounding almost insulted.

"Um, yeah. He's been going out with her all summer."

I feel like I've been zapped, like when you touch something and get that little static jolt, and it takes you a minute to figure out what happened.

"Her name is Amanda. She's in our class." Nate says the word "class" like he means it socially, rather than educationally.

"Oh," is all I manage to say. I wonder if

Livvy knows about Amanda. I wonder if Amanda knows about Livvy. I wonder if going out with Nate is such a good idea.

"So, do you think your parents would let you go if it was Chris and Amanda and you and me?"

"I don't know," I say. At this moment, I don't know a lot of things.

"But you'll ask, right?"

"Yeah, I'll ask."

"Okay. So call me back when you have the answer. The movie is at 7:00. I could pick you up about 6:30." He sounds really excited about this, and I can't figure out why I'm not registering as much enthusiasm as he is.

"As soon as I have the answer," I say. I hang up the phone and stand there, staring at the cupboard where we keep our serving plates and candle holders. *What is wrong with me? This is totally a dream come true, and I am acting like he's asked if I want to willingly infect myself with the plague.*

Mom comes into the kitchen. She has changed out of her work clothes and has on a pair of pale blue shorts and my dad's golf shirt that shrunk in the laundry. "Who was that?"

"Nate," I say. "He wants to know if I can go to a movie tonight with him and his friend Chris."

"Sounds like fun. What show?"

I'm totally stunned at her casual response. I thought I would be lectured. I thought I would be grilled on details. "I didn't ask," I say. "I wanted to make sure it was okay for me to go first."

"As long as it's not an R rating, I don't see why not."

"I'll call back and get the scoop," I say. Instead, I walk up to my room and sit on the edge of the bed, trying to figure out why I feel so weird.

Chapter 10

At 6:25 the doorbell rings. I know it is 6:25 because I have been sitting on the edge of my bed, staring at the clock and trying to keep my stomach from doing its gold medal-winning gymnastics routine.

"Mattie?" Mom's voice has an excitement in it that makes me twice as nervous as before. I check my hair in the mirror again before heading down the stairs. I try to be really low maintenance in the area of hairstyles and make-up. I actually put mascara on tonight, for the first time in about six months. I kept smudging it under my eye and went through half a box of cotton swabs to keep from looking like a raccoon.

". . . home by 11:00, I promise." Nate is talking to my dad. Dad smiles and I take that as a good sign.

"If there's any problem, just give us a call," Dad says. He looks at me and his smile gets bigger. My stomach is going for a perfect ten right now.

"You look really nice," Nate says.

He looks every bit the part of football star. His face is tan, his hair cropped short and combed up in a spiked kind of 'do. His arms are ripped. I mean, chiseled. Like a statue. My knees start the whole gelatin thing, and I suddenly feel like running upstairs and hiding under my bed.

"Thanks," I somehow manage to say. "You look really nice, too." *Spoken like a true twit head.*

"Chris and Amanda are waiting in the car," Nate says. "We should get going so we don't miss the previews."

Dad chuckles like this is some sort of a joke. Mom smiles at me.

Nate opens the door and holds it for me. The Mazda idles in the driveway, and I can't believe I am actually going on a date. A real date. A really and truly real date. A little ticker tape runs through my brain like on the bottom of the screen when you watch CNN. It says, "Don't do anything stupid. Don't do anything embarrassing. Don't act like a dweeb. Don't trip over your shoes." I may look really nice on the outside, but on the inside I'm a complete mess.

I climb into the front seat of the Mazda. Chris and Amanda sit in the back. He nods at me, and she smiles.

"Hi," she says. Amanda is a pretty red-head. She is one of those delicate-looking girls, pale skinned and small boned. Sitting next to Chris's big defensive-back body, she looks like his little sister instead of his girlfriend.

"Hi," I say.

Nate shuts his door. "This is Mattie," he says as he drives off toward the theater.

There is a long line at the box office. We inch our way up to the window behind the other couples, who are trying to pack as much as they can into the final days of summer. Chris has his arm around Amanda. He dwarfs her. She giggles and moves closer to him.

I wonder if Nate will put his arm around me. I wonder if he will kiss me again. I wonder if I should skip the popcorn and stick with chocolate mints, just in case.

"Two for the 7:00," Nate says.

"Fifteen dollars," says the zit-faced guy behind the glass.

I am struck by the sudden fear that I should have brought money with me. *Am I supposed to pay for me? What about dinner? Do I pay for me then?*

Nate hands over a twenty and collects the tickets and his change.

The buttery smell of popcorn wafts through the lobby doors. My mouth waters. There are very few things in the world I love more than movie theater buttered popcorn. Chocolate mints, I remind myself.

"Popcorn?" Nate asks. He puts his arm around my waist and maneuvers me toward the concession line. His hand is warm and sends a chill through my air-conditioned skin. I try not to shudder. I don't want him to think I don't want his arm around me.

"Um," I say. I'm torn.

"With extra butter?"

He's torturing me. I wonder if it's on purpose.

"Sure." I'm weak. I'm completely weak. *What a wimp*. "But I didn't bring my wallet," I say. I'm feeling guilty about the costs associated with taking me out.

Nate laughs. A big, loud laugh that makes people turn and look. I can feel my cheeks burning red, and I try not to run out the nearest exit.

"It's a date," he says. "My treat, you know?"

"Thanks," I say. *Could I be more of a dork?*

Chris and Amanda lead the way. They head to the top of the theater, almost the back row. Nate and I follow, but Nate takes a left and sits across the aisle from Chris. My heart is in a head-to-head competition with my stomach now.

The lights dim and I stare at the screen. Nate slips his arm around my shoulder again and moves closer to me. Previews flash across the screen, but I can't focus on them.

Nate leans closer and whispers, "You look totally hot." My heart tries to climb out my throat, and I am sure that the people in the front row are going to turn around and tell me to be quiet.

"Thanks," I manage to say in almost a croak.

I hear a giggle that I know belongs to Amanda. I want to turn and look, but I am frozen in my seat. *I am so totally in over my head.*

Aliens try to blast Earth to bits on screen. Nate grabs a handful of popcorn from the tub I hold firmly in my lap. I wonder what I am supposed to do. Do I lean over and put my head on his shoulder? Do I bury my face in his chest and pretend to be afraid of the guys in rubber suits on screen? Do I sit here, frozen like a statue in the Geek Hall of Fame? I focus so much on what I should, or shouldn't, be doing that I pay almost no attention to the movie.

The thing is, this isn't how I pictured my first date. For one, Livvy should be here. For another, well, I don't know what the "another" should be, but this isn't how I thought it would work.

More giggling, followed by perturbed "shhh" sounds.

"Get a room," Nate says in a loud whisper.

"Shhh."

I sneak a look over my shoulder. Chris nuzzles Amanda's neck. She must be really ticklish.

"You know what they say," Nate whispers in my ear. "If you can't beat 'em, join 'em."

I turn to look at him, not sure exactly what he means. Then it happens. As I'm turning my head, he leans in to kiss me and—smack—we bang heads.

"Ouch," I say. I grab for my forehead and the bucket of popcorn tumbles out of my hands and spills down the necks and arms of the people in front of me. Then I start to laugh. I can't help it. I didn't know he was going to kiss me, and the fact that we head-butted seems so classically dorky to me, I start to giggle. Nate starts to snicker, too.

"Shhh."

The guy I just baptized with popcorn turns and glares at Nate. This only makes me laugh more, and I clap a hand over my mouth to try and stifle the giggles. The harder I try not to laugh, the more I can't help it.

Nate buries his head in his hands, and I think he's totally embarrassed to be seen with me. My giggles come instantly under control. My first date with Nate will probably be my last one.

I lean over. "I'm sorry," I say. "I didn't mean to . . ."

He's laughing. "It's okay," he says. "Shhh."

"Shhh," I say back.

Nate laughs harder. I get the giggles again. Maybe it's nerves. Maybe I'm a total loser. Is knocking heads and spilling popcorn that funny?

"Shhh," say the people around us.

"Come on," Nate says. He takes my hand and leads me, still giggling, out of the theater. We hit the lobby and both bust out laughing.

"I'm sorry," I say again.

"What for?"

"I don't know. For making you miss the movie?"

"It's totally lame," he says. "That was just too funny, though."

"What, that we clobbered each other?"

"Yeah," he says, then draws a deep breath. "I mean, I'm trying to be so suave, and you're, like, totally into this movie . . ."

"Oh, not at all," I say. Lame is not a strong enough word for this film.

"And then, wham." Nate bangs his fists together and starts laughing again. "And the popcorn goes all over that guy, and he's staring at me."

"I'm sorry."

"You keep saying that. There's nothing to be sorry for. That was classic."

We sit on one of the cushioned benches in the lobby. A few last giggles escape, and I realize that I'm not feeling like such a loser anymore.

"So what should we do now?" I ask. *Not that I mind sitting here with Nate doing nothing.*

"Let's see if Chris and Amanda come out. Maybe we can go get pizza or something."

I lean over and rest my head on Nate's shoulder. Then I realize what I'm doing and I sit up fast.

"Why'd you move? I was enjoying that."

My heart does one, perfect flip, then

settles back where it belongs. I scooch
over a little closer and rest my head on his
shoulder again. It feels good. Better than I
imagined.

Sooner than I would like, Chris and
Amanda emerge from the theater.

"Dude, this movie totally sucks," Chris
says.

Nate stands and the sudden lack of his
body is like a blast of cold air. "Yeah, let's
bail."

For a moment I think he is going to
walk out and completely forget that I came
with him. Then he turns, holds out his
hand, and helps me up from the bench. He
holds my hand all the way to the car. He
opens the door for me and then holds my
hand while we drive—except when he
needs to shift gears. I make a mental note
to be sure my first car has an automatic
transmission.

Nate pulls into the Medieval Pie pizzeria
and we order the Camelot special. We all
laugh. We all eat pizza. We hold our own
pinball game tournament, which I lose
dreadfully but have more fun at than anyone.

We pile into the Mazda and take Chris and Amanda home. Then it's just the two of us. Me and Nate. Me and the guy I have dreamed about for the better portion of my life. We pull into my driveway, and I am hit by a sudden anger at the word "curfew."

"I had a great time tonight," Nate says.

"Me, too."

"I'm really glad you're going with me on Friday."

"Me, too."

"I really want to kiss you."

"Me, too."

This time there is no banging heads. This time there is only soft, warm lips that brush mine and send tingles through my whole body that don't stop until they reach my toes. There is a warm hand on my cheek. Nate looks at me, his eyes lowered just enough that he looks even more gorgeous than I have ever imagined him.

"You'd better get inside. I don't want your dad to get mad at me."

His words are like a shot of cold water.

"If I keep you out too late," he says, "he won't let me take you out again."

He kisses me again, and my whole body feels warm inside.

It takes all my focus to pull back and reach for the door handle. "I had a really fun time with you."

"Me, too," he says.

Chapter 11

Post-First-Date Pop Quiz

I don't know if you can imagine being me right now, because I'm having a hard enough time imagining being me, and I *am* me. So here's the situation: You come home from your first really real date, which you are sure will never be exceeded in the annals of first-date history. You head to your room to spend the rest of the night reliving the whole thing and discover a note on your door. Your best friend called. The note says you are supposed to call her back, no matter how late. Considering that it is her brother that you just went on your date with, do you:

A. disregard the note because you want to spend your remaining waking moments of the day thinking about how good your life is right now;

B. call your friend and quickly say you'll talk to her in the morning with all the details; or

C. pick up the phone, then hang it up, then pick it up again, then hang it up again, and wonder why this is making you feel so weird.

Yeah, you know which one. I pick up the receiver, listen to the dial tone, then hang up. Then I pick it up again—determined to call—and then hang up even faster than before.

This is so weird. What am I supposed to do? If I call now, Nate will be walking in the door, and he'll think I'm a big blabbermouth who had to call and tell his sister everything about our date. If I don't call, I run the risk of Livvy being even more mad at me than she is now for having gone out with her brother.

Why is it that for every good thing that happens, I have to have something bizarre happen? I decide that the universe conspires against teenage girls in this manner for its own amusement. I don't want Livvy any more upset at me, but I don't want to look like an immature blabbermouth either. *Why me?*

The solution arrives in the form of my dad.

"So, how did it go?"

Other than I nearly fly out of my skin because I didn't hear him come in, I'm glad to see my dad at this moment.

"It was good," I say. "We had fun."

Dad leans against the doorframe, his arms folded across his baggy, white tee shirt. He has on a pair of green sweats that look like two of him could fit in them. *When did you lose so much weight, and how did I not notice?*

"How was the movie?"

I laugh out loud. "It was terrible," I say. "We left early to go get pizza and play pinball." I skip the part about spilling the pop-

corn after banging heads with Nate. I'm
not lying—I'm just not revealing all the
information I have in my possession.

"I'm glad you had a good time." Dad
straightens up, and I wonder if I'm about to
get lectured on something. "It's late,
though, so you'd better get to sleep. You're
mom's got to work tomorrow, and you'll
need to be up early to take care of Donny."

Ah, yes, the killer of all good things.
The mention of my little brother shoots a
big hole in the bubble of joy in which I
have been floating. I roll my eyes and let
out a long sigh.

"It shouldn't be too hard tomorrow,"
Dad says. "He still isn't feeling well, so he'll
probably spend most of the day watching
movies or TV."

"Whatever," I say. "I'm going to bed."

"Good night, beautiful." Dad puts his
arms out, and I move in for a hug. He kisses
the top of my head. It's funny how different
kisses can be, depending on who you're getting them from and the circumstances in
which you're getting them.

I change into my favorite, jumbo-sized

tee shirt, hit the light, and crawl in bed. As
I drift off to sleep, I decide I will call Livvy
first thing in the morning.

* * *

I wake up with the taste of stale popcorn in
my mouth and realize I went to bed without brushing my teeth. I head immediately
for the bathroom to rectify the situation.
Once my teeth have been de-kernelled, I
head to the kitchen to see what Donny's
status is. The house is quiet. No movie
playing, no television droning, no barking.

I go upstairs and check in Donny's
room. He's still sleeping, the blanket pulled
up over his head with only his nose poking
out. He can't stand to have his nose covered. Livvy is convinced it's because he was
smothered in a past life. I think it's just
because he's weird.

Livvy.

I head to my room. I look at the phone.
Instead of calling, I decide I need to get
dressed and brush my hair. I return from
the bathroom, sit on the edge of the bed,
and stare at the phone as if it will tell me

what to do.

"I can't call from here," I say. "I might wake up Donny and he needs his sleep."

Feeling a little justified in the further delay, I go back to the kitchen and fix a bowl of cornflakes. I lean against the counter, shoveling cereal into my mouth and staring at the phone. *Oh for pity sake, just call her.* With my bowl emptied and rinsed, I decide I've procrastinated long enough. I dial the number.

"Did you have a good time last night?" It's Livvy. She sounds irked.

"Hello to you, too," I say.

"Did you meet Amanda?"

"Is that what this whole attitude is about?" I say. I'm a little miffed that she is being so snarky at me if she is really just ticked that Chris has a girlfriend that isn't her.

There is silence on the other end.

"Are you still there?" I ask.

"Did you meet her?"

I let out a sigh. "Yeah. I met her."

"And."

"And what? She's a twit head." A little

twinge of guilt plucks at my heart because I don't really think Amanda is a twit head. I thought that at first, but during pizza and pinball, I discovered that she is really sweet and very smart.

"So why is Chris going out with her, then?"

I sigh again. "How should I know? Maybe he likes dim-witted redheads."

The little twinge gets a little bigger.

"So, did you have a good time?"

"Yes," I say in a flat voice.

"It's not supposed to be this way."

I'm not sure I want to get into this conversation right now, but before I can think it through, I'm into it up to my ankles. "What's not supposed to be what way?"

"You know what I mean."

"No, Livvy, I don't. What do you mean?"

"We're supposed to be going out together. You're dumping me as your friend so you can go out with my brother. Do you know how that makes me feel? It's like this whole time you've been my friend just so you could get this shot, and now that it's happened, you don't need me anymore. Do you know how that feels? Can you even imagine how that makes me feel?"

Livvy unloads on me like an overfilled dump truck. I wait for her to take a breath.

"What am I supposed to do?" I ask. "Tell Nate I can't go out with him because Chris won't go out with you?"

"Isn't that what real friends do for each other?"

My face gets hot, and I realize that I am gripping the phone so tight it's hurting my hand. "Aren't real friends supposed to be excited for each other when something good happens?" I grit my teeth and wait for the next volley to be launched.

"So, I guess we don't have much of a friendship then."

Before I can respond, the line goes dead. I slam the phone down and let out an exasperated yell.

"Momma," Donny cries from upstairs. Now I'm really ticked. Not only did my now ex-best friend hang up on me, but she made me wake up my annoying brother.

"Momma," he cries again.

"Mom's at work. You're stuck with me."

Donny shuffles into the family room, dragging his ratty blanket behind him. He crawls onto the sofa and curls up in a ball. "Sesmee Stweet," he says.

I look for the remote and turn on the PBS station. "Dragon Tales," I say.

"Sesmee Stweet," he whines.

"It's not on right now," I say. "It's Dragon Tales."

Donny starts to cry.

"Donny, it's not on right now. It will be on later." The pitch of my voice is climbing some invisible ladder. I throw the remote on the counter and stomp up to my room. I know it's not Donny's fault that I'm upset, but I can't stand it when he whines. It's like nails on a chalkboard.

I use Mom's "deep breath and count to ten" routine to calm down, then I go back to see if Donny wants breakfast. He is still curled up in a ball on the sofa, but he's asleep again. *This is just weird.*

He sleeps most of the day, barely moving. He turns down my offer of a grilled cheese sandwich. The weirdest part is his collar. His ever-present shiny red collar is

not present. I find it on the floor in his
closet. When I offer to put it on him and
make his hair spiky again, he doesn't even
respond.

Donny is acting very strange, and my
best friend is now my ex-best friend. All of
this on the heels of perhaps the best night
of my life. I decide I can't focus on the neg-
ative stuff because it will just make me
grumpy. Instead, I get all the laundry done
and wash the dishes. It keeps my mind off
the thing with Livvy and kills the time
until Mom gets home from work.

She looks tired—more tired than
usual—when she comes in from the bakery.

"What's wrong?" I ask.

"I had a long day, and Donny had a
rough night."

I'm surprised. "I didn't hear anything."

"He came into my bedroom about 2:00,
complaining that his heart hurt."

"That's weird," I say. "What was it?"

Mom puts her purse on the counter and
runs a hand through her hair. It catches on
the hair net, which she pulls off. "I think
he meant his chest felt tight. I took him

into my bathroom and steamed him for almost an hour."

"So why don't you go take a nap? You look like you need one."

Mom gives me a wilted smile. "You're a sweetheart, but I'm okay. I want to keep an eye on Donny."

"I can keep an eye on him," I say. After all, he hasn't moved all day, and it's not like he's going to get up and start tap dancing on the ceiling.

Mom leans against the counter and rests her head in both hands. "Maybe I'll take you up on that."

She climbs the stairs and disappears down the hallway, still clutching the hair net in one hand. I decide to live up to the sweetheart label, and I look through the freezer for something to thaw out for dinner. I haven't cooked in a few weeks, and tonight might be a good chance to earn a few more points with the parents. There's a frozen lasagna that looks pretty easy, and I pull it out and set it on the counter. I check the fridge for lettuce and decide to make a salad later.

Dad gets home around 5:00, just as Mom wakes up from her nap. Donny hasn't moved from the sofa. At one point I even went over to be sure he was still breathing. He's really starting to scare me.

Mom manages to get him to eat a little of the lasagna, but not really enough to feed a bird. It's quiet around the dinner table.

"Why isn't he getting better?" I ask as we clean off the table.

Mom rinses dishes in the sink and stacks them in the dishwasher. "The pediatrician said it's just a bug. It'll take a few days to run its course, and then he'll be back to normal."

"That just doesn't seem right," Dad says. "He acts like he feels worse." Dad covers the leftover salad with plastic wrap and sets it in the fridge.

"There's nothing more we can really do," Mom says. There is a sharpness in her voice that tells me she is frustrated and worried. "They don't want him on antibiotics if it isn't bacterial, and his fever is still low-grade, so they want him to fight the bug off by himself and build his immune system."

"Well, if he isn't better by this weekend, I say we take him back to the doctor." Dad sounds almost as frustrated as Mom, but we're all kind of at a loss knowing what to do next. Something definitely isn't right, but nobody knows what. And if the doctor doesn't even know, how are *we* supposed to deal with it?

I think about Donny, laying on the sofa in a fetal position. There is this ache in my heart that scares me. I can't stand seeing my brother like this and feeling so helpless about it. If this is what if feels like just being the sister, I can only imagine how hard it is for my parents. I add this ache to the list of reasons I will never have my own kids.

Chapter 12

It's Friday. It's 5:30 p.m. I'm a nervous wreck.

Nate should to be here in 30 minutes. I have gone through three outfits, two hairstyles, and four pair of shoes. I'm still not dressed. I wish Livvy were here to help me. She would pick out the right clothes, with the right shoes, and fix my hair.

But Livvy isn't speaking to me. No matter how many times I call and leave a message, she doesn't call back. I'm on my own, and I don't trust myself to be me.

After reviewing the choices laid out on my bed for the umpteenth time, I finally settle on a denim skirt, white cotton shirt, and tan sandals. I pin my bangs back from

my forehead and decide I look like I'm
twelve. I opt for the gold headband with
the pink rhinestone flowers on it. I brush
my eyelashes with mascara, and I even put
a little blush on my cheeks. *This is so not
me.* I brush my teeth for the third time
today. My dentist is going to lose money on
me this year.

The doorbell rings at 5:55, and I can't
decide if I am angry that I don't have the
extra five minutes or relieved that I don't
have to spend them worrying about what
doesn't look right. It's too late now. Nate's
at the door.

"Mattie, Nate's here," my dad calls from
downstairs. I take a deep breath and let it
go slowly. I can't figure out why I am so
nervous. I mean, we went out two nights
ago and it was fine. So what's the issue
now? Is it that this is like a public
announcement that we're going out? Is it
that everyone and their dog will be at
school? Is it because Livvy is the only person who won't be there?

The universe can be very cruel to
teenage girls. I try to calm myself down.

Just think of it as another night without Donny duty.

"Wow, you look really great," Nate says as I step into the hallway. He looks incredibly yummy himself. Denim shorts and a black golf shirt. There's a gold chain around his wrist.

My heart has been replaced by the hummingbird again. I hope my knees don't buckle and send me sprawling on the floor.

Dad looks out the door at the Mazda in the driveway. "You really did a nice job with the car," he says. "Sounds like it's running well."

"Yeah. Thanks for your help. My dad is totally worthless at car stuff." Nate gets that "awe, shucks" look on him, and I half expect him to kick at some invisible rock on the ground.

"Hey, anytime," Dad says. I know he means it, too. A few weeks ago I would have cringed at his offer. Now I'm glad that my dad likes my date and my date likes my dad. Maybe the universe is trying to make up for the other stuff.

"Home by midnight," Dad says.

I'm thinking I should scoop my jaw back up off the floor where it has fallen. *Midnight?* I'm not going to say anything because if this is a dream, I don't want it to end.

Dad flips his wallet out of his back pocket and starts sorting through bills.

"Oh, no bother Mister James. I've got it covered." Nate holds his hand up in protest.

"You're sure?" Dad looks from the money in his hand to Nate, then back at the money.

"Yeah, really."

Dad puts the wallet back, and there is a strange sense of relief that surges through me. I smile at my dad.

Nate opens the door and I turn to follow. I feel a hand on my wrist, then Dad presses a piece of paper into my hand. I look to see what it is. It's a twenty. I look at Dad, smile and mouth "thank you," then head toward the midnight blue Mazda. It's empty.

"Where are Chris and Amanda?" I ask. *Not that I really care.*

"They're meeting us at the dance."

I'm technically on my first *solo* date, which isn't supposed to happen yet. The guilt instilled in me by years of good parenting starts to rear its ugly head, and I wonder if I should go back and let my dad know. Then I wonder if that's why he was checking out the car so closely, noticing that nobody else was in it, and that he knew it was a violation, but he let me get away with it anyway. I'm very confused. I decide that I will not say anything about it unless asked, and then I'll tell them that we met up with everyone else at school. After all, it's only a five-minute drive.

"So what do you say we go get something to eat before we go?"

Okay, maybe it's going to be more than five minutes.

"Um, yeah, sure." *All the charm of a garden slug.*

"Your choice," Nate says. He looks over at me, shifting the car to another gear. "You really do look great."

I'm blushing. I can feel the heat rushing to my cheeks, and I wonder if putting makeup on will actually make this worse.

"So, where do you want to go?" He reaches over and takes my hand in his.

"I don't know," I say. I really don't. Suddenly I can't think of the name of any restaurant or fast food place. I don't know what's close by. I don't know what they serve. All I know for certain is that my face is getting warmer by the second, and I'm really not all that hungry.

"Is Roller Burger okay? They have great onion rings."

Yes, good, a name. "Yeah, Roller Burger sounds great."

We sit in the Mazda and wait for a blonde girl on roller skates to make her way to our window. She doesn't look all that stable. On the skates, I mean. She gets the order, then repeats it back to make sure she didn't miss anything. Then she skates off to the kitchen.

"I had a really good time with you the other night," Nate says. He takes off his seat belt and turns sideways. He looks very good in black.

"I did, too," I say. I wonder if I'm drooling.

"I'm really glad you said you'd come with me tonight. I thought maybe Livvy would try to talk you out of it."

Livvy. My brain races. Should I tell him that she did try to talk me out of it? Should I blow it off like it was no big deal?

"Um, well . . ." I'm so not sure what to say here.

"She did, huh?" He isn't so much asking as confirming. "I thought she would. She just doesn't get it."

Get what? I look up at the roof of the car. I look at my hands folded in my lap. I don't look at Nate. I wonder if I have really lost my best friend over this guy. If so, is it worth it? I mean, so far I think it is, but so far is only three days. Compare that with—what—six years? But then, I've known Nate that long, too. Does that count though? He wasn't even aware that I was a member of the same species until just a week ago.

"Hello? Are you in there?" Nate waves his hand in front of my face.

"Sorry," I say. "I got a little distracted for a minute."

"Yeah, I guess so. I thought maybe you slipped into a coma or something."

Ha ha—ouch—wait a minute. "Well, this

whole thing has really shaken Livvy up, and I feel really weird about it. I mean, she's been my best friend for, I don't know, six years I guess." *Help, I'm babbling and I can't shut up!* "I know she wants me to be happy, but I guess she thought maybe she would be around to share in it, and when it didn't happen the way we thought, it kind of freaked her out."

It dawns on me that I probably would have understood this sooner if I hadn't been so caught up in my own stuff. Maybe that's why Livvy can't be happy for me, because she's caught up in her own stuff. We definitely need to sit down and sort through our stuffs before Monday. I can't start the school year without my best friend being my best friend.

"It's like I said," Nate says, intruding on my thought process. "Livvy isn't like you. She's a total dork."

"No," I say, and I am surprised at how firm my voice comes out. "She isn't a total dork. She isn't a partial dork. There is nothing dork-like about her—except maybe how bad she has it for Chris. But if that's what makes her a dork, then I'm just as big a dork as she is, because that's how bad I've had it for you forever."

Well, maybe Guinness will want this one for the "shortest romance in history" section.

Nate looks stunned. Literally. Like someone just dumped ice water down his shorts, and he isn't exactly sure how to respond.

But I'm on some sort of self-destructive roll, and I can't find the off switch, so I keep going. "You know, if you gave her half a chance, you'd see that she's one of the coolest human beings on the planet. She's the most creative person I know, and one of the funniest, too. She is a genius when it comes to stuff like which shirt goes with which skirt. My little brother won't have a thing to do with me, but he'll kill or die for your sister."

Nate's eyes have gotten so big that I wonder if it's possible they might pop out of his skull.

"I really like you, Nate."

He stares at me. I think I've scared him.

"But if we're going to go out, it means

you can't bad-mouth your sister around me. She is my best friend. I wouldn't let anybody else bad mouth her, so I definitely won't let you." I take a deep breath, then let it out in a louder-than-expected sigh. "If that means you won't go out with me anymore—well—then that's what it means." Nate leans against the door like a man who has been shot multiple times, but still can't believe it happened.

The blonde girl on skates comes teetering toward the car, a large tray balanced precariously on her shoulder. Nate doesn't see her coming, and when she knocks on the window, he levitates at least six inches off the seat of the car. The blonde on skates is so startled that she starts to topple over, back, then forward, then—in a mighty tidal wave of sodas, onion rings, napkins and straws, the whole tray launches through the window, down Nate's shirt, over the stick shift, and into a tidal pool on my denim skirt.

The blonde girl screams incoherently as she stumbles off in tears. Nate holds his arms up in a form of surrender, soda dripping down his neck.

Once again the universe has conspired against me, and the only thing I can do—is laugh. I slap a hand over my mouth and try to contain it, but there is no stopping the flood of giggles that has welled up inside.

Nate looks like a raging bull, ready to tear to shreds the first thing that gets in its way. He opens the car door and gets out, shaking his soggy shirt and brushing the gooey crumbs from his shorts. He stomps his feet and mutters something.

I open my door, giving in to the giggles that have become full-blown chuckles now. As I stand, the pool of soda splashes off my skirt into a puddle on the ground. Ice cubes swirl on the asphalt and begin to melt.

I steal a glance at Nate, expecting to see his face as red as the cherry that landed on the dashboard.

He smiles. He points at my skirt and starts laughing.

"Now what?" I ask when I can breath again. I look down. It looks frighteningly like I've wet myself, and that makes me start to laugh even harder.

"Well, they better be buying our dinner

is all I have to say," he says.

"No way. It was your fault."

Nate throws his head back in exaggerated shock. "What?"

"You scared the poor girl, and that's why she dumped the tray on you."

"She scared me when she banged on the window."

"It wasn't a bang, it was a tap."

"Sounded like a bang to me." Nate lifts one leg and shakes it, then the other. He is still laughing, and even though he is soggy, he still looks very good in black.

Chapter 13

The manager from Roller Burger offers his profuse apologies while two employees—minus skates—mop up the Mazda. He does not offer to buy our dinner, so we decide it's better if we head somewhere else. We stop off at Nate's house first so he can change clothes. I follow him in through the garage.

"What happened to you?" Livvy asks. She sits on a stool at the counter drinking a glass of lemonade. I smile and laugh at the irony.

"We are still debating that," I say. "My take is that Nate scared the ju-ju-bees out of the waitress at Roller Burger, which caused her to baptize us both in ice-cold drinks and onion rings."

Livvy gives me a little smile, which quickly fades. "Sounds like something Butthead would do."

"His theory," I continue, "is that the waitress startled him first, so it's really her fault that we got drenched and not his."

"Of course it's not his fault," Livvy says. The sarcasm in her voice is as obvious as the big wet spot on my skirt. "Nothing is ever Nate's fault."

"Hey," I say.

"Is for horses," Livvy answers.

"Very funny."

Livvy gulps the rest of her lemonade. "Not a very good start to your date."

"Oh well," I say, because I can't come up with anything better.

"So what, now you're not going? Or did Butthead just decide he needed to torture me over the fact that you have a date, and I don't."

"You know," I say, "it's no wonder he talks about you like he does when you talk about him like this."

"Excuse me?"

"The whole reason we got drenched is

because I told Nate he couldn't bad-mouth you around me if we were going to keep dating. I told him you were my best friend and I wouldn't let anyone else talk about you that way, so why should I let him." *Help, I'm babbling again.* "And I told him that if it meant we couldn't go out anymore because he couldn't stop bad-mouthing you, then too bad and that was okay with me."

Livvy looks a little bit like Nate did—eyes wide, jaw slack. I can feel the heat rushing to my face, and I figure I'm on a roll again. "So now," I continue, "I'm going to tell you the same thing. Your brother has been nothing but nice to me, and I'm not going to let you sit here and call him names because you're mad at me for going out with him. So if that means I have to stop going out with him, then fine. I will. Because you are that important to me." I take a very deep, shaking breath.

"Um," says Livvy.

I don't say anything.

"Um," says Livvy again.

I really, *really* want to keep going out with Nate, but I will not lose my best friend over it. An idea begins taking shape in the back of my brain. It wiggles its way forward and forms itself into a reasonably good thought.

"Go get dressed and come with us," I say.

"Yeah, right," Livvy says. Again with the sarcasm.

"Seriously," I say. "I thought Chris and Am…er…I thought there were other people coming with us, and I'm not really allowed to go out unless it's a group date. If you come with us, it will be. A group I mean." I'm very pleased at my quick thinking.

"First," Livvy says, leaning back on the counter and folding her arms. "If I really thought you wanted me to come along, I might even give it thirty seconds of consideration. But you don't really want me to. Second, I know for a fact that Nate will have total nuclear meltdown if I go. He'll be just like you, complaining about having to drag the younger sibling everywhere and how it takes all the fun out of things."

Ouch. "I don't complain about Donny that much."

Livvy rolls her eyes. "Again I say—yeah, right."

Ouch!

"Third, and finally, what makes you think I even want to go to the stupid Welcome Back Stomp? Why would I give up one of my last nights of freedom before school starts when I could . . ."

"Sit on your butt in front of the television?" I say.

"I have plans," Livvy says. She sits up straight on the stool.

"Uh-huh."

"I do," she says, louder than before.

"Okay, fine," I say. "You have plans. Sorry I asked."

Livvy slumps back against the counter. "Okay, they may not be as great as your plans, but I did have something to do tonight."

"Laundry?" I ask. I take a step toward her.

"Ha."

"Cleaning your room?" I take another step.

"Doesn't need it," she says.

"Arranging your sock drawer?" I'm standing right in front of her now.

"You are so funny."

I grab her hands in mine. "Please," I say.

"Come with me."

"If it was just you," she says.

"Oh bother about your brother. Forget he's there, and come and have a good time."

"He'll make sure I don't."

"I'll make sure you do."

Livvy sits quietly. She bites her lower lip then looks up at me. "I really want to go," she whispers.

"Then do," I whisper.

"Okay," she says. "But not unless you change your clothes."

We both start to giggle and I feel like a big weight that had been sitting on my shoulders suddenly sprouts wings and flies away.

Nate emerges from his room, wearing khaki shorts and a dark green shirt. He looks very good in green.

"Livvy's coming with us," I say. Nate opens his mouth to say something. I flash him my best "drop the subject or lose a limb" look. He makes the correct decision.

"I'll be down in less than five," Livvy says. "Don't let him drive off without me."

"Thanks a lot," Nate says when Livvy is out of earshot.

"You're welcome a lot," I say.

"Why did you invite her to go with us?"

"Because," I say, "I'm really not supposed to be flying solo yet. I thought Chris and Amanda were coming with us."

"Yeah, well, I arranged it so we would have a little private time."

"Clever boy," I say. "But that's a really good way to make sure I don't get to go out with you again."

"And why is that?"

"Because if my parents find out that I was on a date date, rather than a group date, they would forbid me from going out until I am 37 years old."

Nate steps closer to me and starts to put his arm around my waist. I step back, pointing at my still-damp attire.

"But how would they know? Unless someone told them, and I'm certainly not going to tell them."

"No, but if they ask me, I'll have to tell them."

Nate looks puzzled. He tips his head and his eyebrow scrunches down.

"I can't lie. I'm the world's worst liar. In

fact, if I even think about lying, I am totally busted before I ever get the words from
my brain to my mouth."

"That bites," he says.

"Yes and no." I sit on a stool. "It keeps
me from being sorry or worrying about cov-
ering my tracks."

"Hmmm," is all Nate says.

In less than five minutes (I kept track
on the wall clock), Livvy is ready and we
head for the car.

"It took me an hour to pick out this outfit," I say. "Now I have to find a replacement in five minutes or less."

"Not to worry, chica," says Livvy. "Your
personal fashion consultant is here." She
leans in between the two front seats, and
even though I feel a little awkward, I'm
glad she is here and that she decided to
come to the dance.

We pull into the drive at my house, and
I hit the ground running. Livvy is close on
my heels. "You can come in if you want," I
say to Nate.

"I'll wait here, if it's okay."

"Suit yourself," I say. "I promise I'll hurry."

"I promise, she'll look fabulous," says Livvy.

I look at her. "Thanks," I say.

"What are friends for, chica? Now, dahling, let's get you dressed for the ball."

The house is dark. The front door is locked.

"That's weird," I say, searching for the spare key that Mom hides under the little birdhouse by the walk. I'm a little creeped out by the fact that it appears no one is home. Mom didn't mention she had plans, and neither did Dad. And I can't imagine them going anywhere when Donny is so sick. They wouldn't leave him with a stranger.

"Where is everybody?" Livvy asks.

"That's what I'd like to know."

I flip the light on in the hallway and head toward the den. "Hello?" I call. "Come out, come out, wherever you are."

Nothing.

Livvy climbs the stairs. "Mrs. James? Are you up there?"

"This isn't right," I say, trying to sound casual.

"Maybe they went to a movie."

I shake my head. "Donny's been way too sick. Unless he made a miraculous recovery, which I highly doubt."

"Did they leave you a note?"

I turn and walk toward the kitchen. Mom leaves notes for me on the fridge if she has to leave them.

A yellow piece of scratch paper is stuck to the door of the refrigerator. I pull the apple-shaped magnet away and read the note.

Taking Donny to St. Ben's ER. Will call later. M & D

My hand starts to shake. "Why are they taking him to the ER?"

"Come on, Nate can drive us up there." Livvy puts her arm around my shoulder, but I stand firm. I'm frozen.

"What happened?" I ask.

Livvy takes my shoulders firmly and looks me in the eye. "We don't know until we get there to see what's going on. Let's go get in the car."

My heart beats so hard that it feels like my whole body is shaking.

I'm still gripping the note as I climb

into the Mazda. Nate smiles at me, but his smile wilts when I hand him the note from Mom and Dad.

"What happened?" he asks.

"I don't know."

Livvy leans into the space between us. "We need to go to St. Ben's ER and find her mom and dad."

Nate doesn't say a word. He shoves the car into reverse and squeals the tires as he heads toward the hospital.

Chapter 14

The doors to the emergency room slide open and I quickly scan the waiting area, looking for my parents. A lady comforts a little girl who has her arm in a sling. An older man sits with his head in his hands. A dark-haired man paces back and forth by a window.

"Can I help you?" says a nurse in a flowered scrub shirt.

"I'm looking for Donny," I answer.

She looks at me with a confused smile. "Is that a friend?"

"No," I say, "He's my little brother. My parents brought him in." I try to look over her shoulder and into the treatment area behind her.

"What's the last name?" the nurse asks.
"James."

She types something into the computer, then pauses while the information comes up on her screen. It feels like time has slowed to a crawl while I wait for her to tell me where my brother is.

Nate and Livvy come into the waiting area. Livvy hurries to my side and puts her arm around my waist. I lean my head against her shoulder.

"James, Donald. He's in the Pediatric ICU on the third floor." The nurse looks from the screen to me. "Go through the door over there and down the hall. The elevator is on your right. The third floor nurse can help you out."

We all move toward where she's pointing. The heavy door leads to a dim hallway. Sounds seem muffled and no one talks as we get on the elevator. The nurses' desk is down the hall, and I practically run to get there.

"Excuse me," I say. "I'm looking for my little brother. His name is Donny James. The nurse in the ER told me he was here."

A petite woman with short, brown hair and pale pink scrubs turns from her filing to look at me.

"I'm sorry," she says. "It's past visiting hours. You'll have to come back tomorrow."

"But he's my brother," I say.

"Are Mr. and Mrs. James here?" It's Nate's voice. Calm, low, and in control.

"I'll check and see." The nurse walks off, away from the desk and down a short hall to the left. She slips into a room, keeping the door closed so I can't see anything. When she comes back out a moment later, Mom follows her. Tears flood my eyes and spill down my cheeks. I want to run to Mom, but I hold on to the counter at the desk and wait for her to make her way to me.

"Mattie," Mom starts, but I don't let her finish.

"What's wrong? What happened to Donny?"

Mom has dark circles under her eyes, and I can tell she has been running her hands through her hair a lot. "Donny was having a hard time breathing. We got concerned and brought him to the ER."

"So why is he up here?"

Mom takes my hands in hers. "He has pneumonia. It's pretty bad. All of his left lung is filled with fluid, and his right one is partially filled. He's going to be spending the night here, and maybe a few days more."

"Is he going to be okay?" I feel jittery and weak. If my heart beats any faster, I'm sure it's going to quit working all together. I wipe at my eyes with the back of my hand. "Why can't I go see him? I want to go see him."

"He's sleeping now. The medicines they gave him made him really sleepy, and he needs to rest."

"But Mom, I have to see him," I say. I feel like I'm whining, but I can't help it. I hate feeling this helpless.

"Dad and I are going to stay with him tonight. You can come tomorrow when he's awake."

"Can't I just go peek at him? I won't wake him. I promise. I'll just look through the door."

Mom looks over her shoulder toward the room where my brother is sleeping. She walks away and talks to the nurse in pink.

The nurse looks at me, says something to my mom, then nods her head. Mom comes back.

"You can look in, but you can't go in. Nate and Livvy will have to wait here."

I look at my friends.

"Maybe you can come and stay at our house if your mom and dad are going to be here all night?" Livvy puts her cool hand on my arm.

Nate nods. "I'll go call our mom and ask. You check on your little brother."

I follow Mom to Donny's room. There is only a little light from the panel over his bed. He is sleeping flat on his back, not curled up like a caterpillar. His soft hair is smoothed back off his forehead. A clear tube runs from his nose to a tank labeled "Oxygen" that is attached to the wall behind the bed. The thick plastic rails of the bedside are up. Dad leans on one side, holding Donny's hand in his. Another tube leads from a bag of clear fluid and disappears under a bandage on Donny's arm. There is some little gizmo attached to his finger. Green lights flash on a monitor next to the bed.

Donny looks so small and fragile in the big hospital bed, and I can't figure it out; if this is the pediatric unit, why is he in such a big bed? Dad looks up at me and gives me a faint smile. Tears drip from my cheeks to my shirt, but I don't bother to wipe them. I don't move.

Fluid in his lungs? How did he get fluid in his lungs? From the swimming pool? The life-guard said he probably got water in his lungs. Why didn't I watch him closer? Why didn't I tell Mom sooner how he was acting so sick? Why didn't the doctor see this sooner?

Mom puts her arm around me. I sniff as quietly as I can and slowly back out of the room.

"Is this because of him falling in the pool?" I ask. I'm afraid of the answer, but I'm ready to take full responsibility. If the fluid got in there because of Donny falling in the water on my watch, I will take whatever punishment is necessary for the rest of my life.

"The doctor doesn't think so. That much fluid in his lungs means it's been building up for a longer period of time."

I let out a small sigh.

"But the fall in the pool didn't help," Mom adds.

My heart sinks. "It's my fault, isn't it?"

Mom looks at the floor. "No, Mattie, it's not. I'm sorry if I made you feel that way."

"But you said . . ."

"I'm sorry, Mattie. That's not what I meant."

It doesn't matter what she says now. I know what she meant. She meant that if I hadn't been so irresponsible, Donny wouldn't be so sick.

I will never, never, *take my eyes off Donny again when I watch him, I swear.*

But if this has been building up for a while . . .

"Why didn't the doctor know how sick he was? Why did it take so long for them to find out what it was?" My voice comes out in a harsh whisper.

"There's no rattle," Mom says.

"What rattle?" I say, a little perturbed with Mom's explanation.

"In his chest. Pneumonia usually has a rattling sound that a doctor can hear. This one doesn't."

My brain is spinning. I'm confused and scared and hurt, and I don't know which one to focus on at the moment.

Scared comes in first place.

"Is he going to be okay?"

Mom sighs and runs her hand through her hair. "They've given him a lot of medications to help him breathe and to clear out the infection that's causing this. He's on an IV to give him some extra fluid for his body to keep him from getting dehydrated. We'll know more tomorrow."

This answer doesn't take fear out of first place. In fact, it scares me more. I want to know *now* that Donny is going to be okay. I want to know *now* that he will be jumping on my bed and licking my face—if not tomorrow, then at least in a few days.

I swear, I will never complain about having to take Donny anywhere, as long as he gets well enough to go with me. My prayers are silent, but serious. I think about Livvy's words to me from earlier, saying that I complain all the time about dragging Donny around, about how he gets in the way. I hear my own voice complaining to Mom about having to do everything with my little brother, and I am hit by a wave of guilt that nauseates me. *He's just a little kid. How could I be so mean?*

"I want to stay here. Isn't there a waiting room I can stay in?"

"You can see him in the morning," Mom says softly.

Livvy comes down the hallway. "My mom said it's okay for Mattie to stay. Nate went to get the car."

I look from Livvy to my mom. She gives a relieved smile, but I can see in the creases around her eyes that she is hiding her worry from me. I can't hide my worry. It's the same thing as lying and tears begin flowing again.

"You go with Livvy and then come back in the morning." Mom folds her hands and lets her arms hang, not pushing me away, but not touching me to reassure me.

How can I leave when he's here because of me?

"Come on, Mattie. We'll talk Nate into stopping for food. We can get your stuff and go to my house and watch movies."

I don't move.

"Honey," Mom says.

"Mattie," Livvy says. Her voice matches Mom's for concern and encouragement.

But I can't move.

"If he's here because of me, I'm staying until he goes home."

"You can't," Mom says firmly. "The hospital will only allow Dad and me to be here tonight." She folds her arms and looks me in the eye, but her voice is softer now. "You can come back in the morning. Then Donny will be awake, and we'll know more about how things are going."

"Besides," Livvy adds, "you can't do anything by being here, so you might as well come with me and try to get your mind off it."

Yeah right, get my mind off it.

"I need to get back," Mom says. She puts her arms out, and I step closer and hug her.

"Tell Donny I came to see him, and I'll come back tomorrow."

"I will."

I follow Livvy to the elevator and out of the hospital. Nate drives back to my house so I can grab clean clothes and pajamas. I find Donny's shiny red collar and tuck it in my bag.

We stop to order a replacement dinner but I can't focus on food, and despite the growling in my stomach, I can't eat. Back at Livvy's, we sit on the sofa and flip through the channels in search of something to take our minds off the evening's events. Nate fills in the missing details for his parents, except the part about our discussion of his sister bashing. I don't bother to add this into their talk.

There is a knot the size of a bowling ball in my stomach. I feel like crying, but tears won't come. I want to call the hospital, but I don't want to bug Mom and Dad, or wake up Donny.

Instead, I sit on the sofa with my knees pulled up, clutching a pillow against my body. Around midnight, Livvy declares that she is checking out for the night.

"I'll be up soon," I tell her.

Nate and I sit in silence, him on one end of the sofa, me on the other, watching an old movie musical that neither of us is really interested in.

"Are you gonna be okay?" he says finally.

"I don't know."

He scoots across the cushions and puts his arm around my shoulder. "Hey, it's gonna be all right. You'll see."

"But if it's not . . ." I say.

"It will be."

I don't want to cry in front of Nate. I don't know why, but I feel so stupid crying in front of him when we were supposed to be out dancing tonight. Trying so hard not to cry is an absolute guarantee that I will, which I do, which makes this whole thing seem even worse. As if it could be worse.

"I guess I really messed up our date," I say.

Nate brushes my hair away from my forehead. "Not at all," he says. "There will be other dances."

I wipe my face against my shoulder. "You know, for a butthead, you're a pretty nice guy."

Nate laughs. "Yeah, well, for the best friend of a dork, you're not too bad either."

I laugh. "Hey, can I bug you to do me a favor?"

Nate gives me an exaggerated skeptical look, stretching his mouth down and pulling back from me a bit. "I don't know, you've really tested my generosity tonight."

"I know, I know," I say, a twinge of guilt poking me in the heart. I know he's teasing, but I ruined our date because it's my fault that Donny got sick, and we wound up going to the hospital instead of the stomp, and, oh, never mind. Me and guilt are on a first-name basis tonight.

"I'd do anything for you," Nate says, and my knees start to melt again even though they are pulled up and hugged into my body.

"Could you drive me over to the toy store tomorrow, just really quick, and then take me up to the hospital again?" I feel weird about asking. "I mean, I know you're not my personal shuttle service, but . . ."

"Hey, not a problem." Nate takes my chin in his hand, and I have to look right into his face. I wonder how much of me would be turning to mush right now if I weren't so worried about Donny.

He kisses me. A warm, slick tear slides down my cheek.

"I want to find a present to take to Donny. A stuffed animal."

"Let me get my sunglasses," Nate says as he shades his eyes. "The glare off that halo is really bright."

I smack him on the shoulder, but not hard enough to do anything.

"It's getting late," says Mrs. Byer.

Nate practically lurches across the sofa away from me. I jump at least two inches, maybe three.

Mrs. Byer laughs. "Sorry, I didn't mean to scare you."

Blood rushes to my cheeks, and I wonder how long she's been standing there. Did she see Nate kiss me? Did she see me crying?

"Yeah, okay, thanks, Mom." Nate tries to recapture his cool, which has temporarily fluttered off somewhere. His discomfort in front of his mom makes me even more uncomfortable than before. Now even my ears are burning.

"Okay, so, goodnight. I'll see you in the morning," Nate says. He slides from the sofa, stretches, and trundles off down the hallway toward his room.

"You should get some sleep, Mattie.
Your folks will need your help tomorrow."
Mrs. Byer pats my shoulder, turns, and goes
back up the stairs.

I sit alone in the Byers' front room.
Sleep is about as likely as aliens landing
and offering me the secrets of the universe.
I flip through the channels and finally settle on some infomercial about the latest
miracle diet.

Chapter 15

"Chica."

I bolt into an upright position. I rub my eyes and blink, forcing my brain to focus. "What time is it?"

Livvy plunks down on the sofa where, I just now realize, I fell asleep last night. "It's about 8:30."

"A.M. or P.M.," I ask, only half-joking.

"A.M., you goon."

Donny.

"I gotta hurry," I say.

"What for?"

"I need to do something before I go see Donny."

I jump from the sofa, leaving Livvy as I race to the shower. I want to get to the store and then to the hospital as early as I can. I decide I will call and talk to Mom as soon as I'm dressed, to see how Donny did last night.

I dry my hair with a towel, then realize I didn't bring the clean clothes into the bathroom with me. In fact, I slept in the same outfit that I wore on the disastrous event that was supposed to be a date. I pick up the skirt and sniff.

"Whew," I say. It reeks of onion rings.

I wrap myself in the damp towel I used for my hair, grab my smelly, wrinkled clothes, and head for Livvy's room to get dressed in something that won't offend quite so many people.

I hurry up the stairs to finish getting ready. With my hair dry and clean clothes on, I meet up with Livvy in the kitchen. She is finishing off a bowl of cereal.

"Want some?" she says, then she slurps the last of the milk out of the bowl.

"I don't think I can eat."

"Did you get much sleep? That sofa isn't too comfy."

"Not much," I say. "But I did learn all about the most successful dieting tool of the 21st century." I use my best spokesperson voice.

"I hope it's better than the not-eating-when-you're-stressed plan that you're on right now."

I sink into a chair at the table and put my head in my hands. "I can't help it if I'm not hungry."

"At least have some Vitamin C," she says. She pours two glasses of orange juice and sets one in front of me.

"Thanks."

I sip the cool, tangy juice, feeling it chill me as it works its way down my throat. From nowhere, tears begin to slide down my face. Silent sobs shake my body, softly at first, then growing until I am crying hard, and I don't care who sees me or hears me.

Livvy comes over and puts her arm around me, patting my back. "It's okay, it's okay."

"Can I use the phone?" I say.

"Sure." She grabs the portable off the stand on the kitchen counter.

"I need the phone book, too."

She rummages through a big drawer and pulls out the phone book for me. I flip through pages until I find the listing for St. Benedict's Hospital. I wipe the tears from my face and sniff back the rest of my sobbing. The number for patient information is buried in a long list of numbers for various departments at the hospital.

"I need the room of Donny James," I say, my voice cracking and hoarse.

"One moment," says the female voice. Clicks are followed by beeps.

There is a strange buzzing sound, then, "Hello?"

"Mom?" I say. "Is Donny okay? Is he better? Can I come and see him?"

I'm crying again, and there is a dull ache in my chest that makes me want to jump up and run outside screaming.

"He's a little better today," Mom says. "He's resting right now."

"Is he going to be okay?" I ask between sobs. My hand hurts from gripping the phone so tightly.

"Yes, honey, he's going to be fine. Just

calm down."

"I'm sorry, Mom. I'm so sorry I didn't take better care of him. I'm sorry I didn't see how sick he was and tell you sooner. I should have told you. I should have . . ."

"Mattie, honey, it isn't your fault." Mom's voice is firm but not angry. "The doctor who came in this morning thinks this goes back to the cold Donny had a few weeks ago." She pauses, and I take a sniffling breath, jagged but calmer than before.

"You can come and see him after 10:00 this morning. I can have Dad come and pick you up."

"Nate said he would bring me. We're coming as soon as he finishes his shower."

"That will be good." Mom's voice is soft. "He's been asking about you all morning."

I smile. "Tell him I have a present for him," I say.

"He'll be very excited."

"How are you and Dad?"

Mom sighs. "We're tired. Dad's going to go home and take a shower and then come back to spell me for a bit."

"Maybe you can sneak out when I get

there. Take a little break or something."

"That would be nice," Mom says.

I say goodbye and give the phone back to Livvy.

Nate comes into the kitchen. "Ready when you are, miss."

"What time does the toy store open?" I ask.

"Not until ten, I think, but Target and Wal-Mart are open now." Nate spins the car keys on his finger, then grabs them in his palm.

"Works for me," I say.

Nate looks at Livvy. "Tell Mom and Dad we're taking Mattie. We'll wait in the car for you."

Livvy's eyes grow wide.

"What," Nate says, his voice loud and protesting.

"Nothing." Livvy runs down the hall and yells to her parents that we are leaving.

"Wow," I say to Nate. "That was darn civil of you."

"You tell anyone, especially Chris, and I will deny it ever happened."

I make like I'm zipping my lips. Then I

unzip. "I need to get my stuff."

Livvy and Nate are waiting in the car. I toss my bag on the floor and climb in. "I really appreciate you two," I say. "Really, really."

"Yeah, you're not bad for a toad either," Livvy says.

***

Donny has been moved out of the ICU and is in a room with another bed in it. Mom waves at me to come in, and I slip through the door quietly. There are still tubes in his nose and arm, and monitors beeping and flashing by the bedside.

"Donny," I say.

He sits up a little and opens his eyes.

"Mattie," he says.

Mom moves out of the chair, and I sit next to the bed.

"Hey little guy, how are you feeling?"

Donny wrinkles his face and sticks his tongue out.

"That good, huh?"

A fit of coughing wracks his little body for a moment, and the ache in my heart starts up again.

"I go home wiff you?"

"I don't know. We'll have to ask the doctor. But pretty soon, I'm sure. Pretty soon." I'm not really sure. I'm not sure of anything except that I feel like a total schmuck. Even if this isn't my fault, even if he was sick before, I let him fall in the pool, I've been a rotten big sister.

"What dat?" Donny says. He spots the bag I have tried to hide behind my back.

"Oh, that?" I say, teasing him. "That's nothing."

"It my pwesent," he says.

"Nope, no present here," I say.

"It my pwesent," he says again, more confident than before.

I smile at him. "You wanna open it?"

He nods, but he starts coughing again. I look at Mom to see how concerned she is. Only a little anxiety rests at the corner of her eyes. I decide that if she isn't more worried, I won't be. I don't want to scare Donny any more than he already has been.

I hold out the bag for him.

Donny grabs the sack from me and pulls all the tissue paper out, throwing it to the

floor. Then he pulls out the stuffed, shaggy
sheep dog wearing the shiny red collar.
Donny's eyes flash a brightness that I
haven't seen for what feels like forever. He
hugs the toy, squeezing it against his chest,
and grinning from ear to ear.

"Do you like him?" I ask.

Donny looks at me, saying nothing.

"Do you like him?" I ask again.

Donny smiles.

"Arf."

I lean over, hugging him gently, careful
not to bump the clear tubes attached to his
arm. He hugs my neck so hard I almost
can't breath, but I don't care. The door
opens and a tall nurse wheels in a tray. I
hold the toy dog while Donny nibbles at
his lunch and Mom nags at him to use his
fork. I secretly wish he would get on all
fours and lick the plate. Soon his eyes
grow heavy.

"I know he's glad you came," Mom says
as I stand to leave.

"Tell him I'll be back later," I say.

Nate and Livvy are watching TV in the
visiting lounge. I flop on the sofa between

them and wrap an arm around each of them.

"Thanks for waiting," I say. "I guess we can head out now."

"How's he doing?" Nate asks.

"Sleeping now. He seems to be doing okay, though. I'm going to come back with my dad later on."

We stand and start walking down the hallway, me in the middle of my best friend and—dare I think it?—my boyfriend.

Livvy squeezes my hand. "Are you okay?" she asks.

I squeeze back and answer, "Arf."

About the Author

Kim Justesen lives in Sandy, Utah, just 15 minutes away from where she grew up, with her husband Mike and her three children, Morgan, Ryan, and Amanda. She also mothers a dog, two cats, and a hermit crab. Kim earned a Master's Degree in Writing from Vermont College and teaches college English part-time. When she isn't grading English papers, she enjoys knitting and crocheting.

Tell us what you think!

Hey chicas (and chicos)! Did you love this book? Did you hate this book? Tanglewood Press is here for you—to publish the books you want to read. But we want to make sure we're doing it right. So we want your help!

Here's what you'll get:

- To the first 500 people who join: a paper dog collar with your choice of tags. If you don't have a brother or sister to wear it, you can use it as a bookmark. If you're not in the first 500, we'll tell you how you can get one anyway!

- Membership in our focus group. You'll help us decide what books to publish!

- Advance notice of books that are coming out in the stores or authors coming to your area.

- Chance to get your name in one of our books by participating in some contests that we will announce from time to time— things like coming up with a good book title or book cover.

We hope it's fun for you, but we are serious about wanting your opinions: what you like, what you don't like, what you want in a book, and what you don't want. So come join us!

Here's how. First, you need to get permission from a parent or guardian to do this. Hey, it won't kill you.

Then, go to www.tanglewoodbooks.com and follow the links to My *Brother the Dog* and the Readers Focus Group. You will fill out a very simple questionnaire, asking for your name, your mailing address, your e-mail, and some questions about what you like and don't like to read. That's it!

We want you (and the adults) to know that we will NEVER share your personal information with anyone. This information is just between you and us, period.

Join now and get your dog collar!
Remember: www.tanglewoodbooks.com